GODFATHER OF THE BRIDE: A NOVELLA

AN ANNABELLE ARCHER WEDDING PLANNER MYSTERY #14

LAURA DURHAM

BROADMOOR BOOKS

For Gillian,
whose wicked sense of humor and spirit of adventure have kept me sane
(and laughing) for years and years

CHAPTER 1

"**I** have to say, Annabelle," my assistant, Kate, said as she sat with her feet up on my glass coffee table and took a sip of champagne. "I could get used to wedding days like this."

"Well, don't," I told her, swigging my cold, bottled Mocha Frappuccino. "This is not a normal wedding day."

Evidenced by the fact that my assistant wore shorts that would make Daisy Duke blush, I thought, trying not to be distracted by her long, tan legs. On any normal wedding day, we'd both be in appropriate black dresses. At least mine would be appropriate. Kate's would show a little too much leg, but it would be black. This, however, was no normal wedding day.

Kate cast a glance toward my high living room windows where the bride sat on a tall stool getting her hair and makeup done. Late morning light streamed through the glass and glinted off the collection of hairspray cans and makeup palettes laid out on my dining room table. The scent of high-end hair product hung in the air along with the faintest hint of Bengay.

She dropped her voice. "You mean because it's a Friday wedding, and the bride is over eighty, and we're actually in the wedding party instead of running the day?"

"That's part of it." I took another swig of my cold coffee and reminded myself that I really didn't need any more caffeine.

"Does the other part have to do with you not having a wedding day schedule?" Kate asked, the corner of her mouth turning up.

I looked longingly at her champagne. "I'm doing just fine without a schedule."

Kate leaned forward. "Is your left eye twitching?"

I touched a finger to it and shot her a look. "Very funny."

As the owner of Wedding Belles, one of Washington, DC's top wedding planning firms, I was used to running weddings with the precision of a Swiss timepiece. That meant that each wedding had a carefully crafted timeline that outlined the wedding day minute to minute from the moment the bride started getting ready to the time the last vendor loaded out at the end of the event. This wedding, however, was different.

I glanced over at Leatrice, my octogenarian downstairs neighbor, who sat perched on the stool in a Wonder Woman bathrobe, with a tiny brown-and-black Yorkie on her lap. My eyes then went to Fern, my go-to hairstylist, as he teased the back of the bride's jet-black hair.

"I thought we agreed not to make her hair too big," I said, coughing as Fern unleashed a torrent of hairspray.

Fern waved a hand in front of his face. "I have to have volume, sweetie. We're channeling a vintage look."

One look at Fern's own outfit was proof of that. Fern loved nothing more than dressing for the occasion, and especially if the occasion was a wedding. He'd done wedding hair wearing everything from a sari, to a kimono, to leather chaps and a cowboy hat. Today he'd chosen pleated beige pants and a brown, buttoned-up cardigan. He'd even tucked the end of his dark ponytail into the back of the cardigan.

"Are you going for a Mr. Rogers vibe?" I asked.

Fern inhaled audibly. "I'll have you know, this was a very stylish look in the fifties. Of course, I'll be changing for the wedding. I wouldn't dream of performing the ceremony in anything less than my full liturgical attire."

Leatrice rubbed her hands together. "I've always wanted a wedding blessed by a priest."

"He's not a priest," I mumbled. "He was ordained online."

Fern ignored me and leaned down to Leatrice. "Don't you worry. Your wedding is getting the full Fern treatment." He winked at her. "Just wait until you see my cassock and cross."

The Yorkie, named Hermés, yipped in Leatrice's lap. I opened my mouth to say something, then shut it.

"So he's impersonating a priest," Kate said, crossing one bare leg over the other. She tapped a finger to the pale-blue pillbox hat topping her blond bob. "It's not the first time. You and I are playing the part of TWA stewardesses, I mean, bridesmaids."

"Not willingly," I whispered.

She took another drink of champagne. "Our baby-blue suits are better than those orange lace jumpsuits she originally wanted."

Kate had a point. We'd talked Leatrice out of having a disco-themed wedding. We'd also talked her out of an Age of Aquarius motif and had convinced Fern that a murder mystery themed wedding was too on the nose.

"But do you have to wear the hat now?" I asked.

Kate adjusted the boxy hat so it tilted on her head. "Come on. It's fun. I'm getting into the spirit of the wedding. I'm also reveling in the fact that we aren't in charge."

Even though we were wedding planners, Fern had volunteered to plan Leatrice's wedding for her. After a bumpy start, everything had gone smoothly. Relatively speaking. This was due to the fact that Leatrice and her fiancé, Sidney Allen, wanted a small wedding, and because I'd been secretly going behind Fern's back and fixing things.

I knew he'd be offended if he found out, so Leatrice had promised not to breathe a word to anyone. But she'd secretly given me all the contracts before she signed them so I could point out potential pitfalls. I'd also fed vendor names to Leatrice so she could ask Fern about them and used my professional pull to get almost the entire wedding at cost. Of course, it helped that Leatrice had agreed to a Friday afternoon in July when no one in their right mind wanted to get married. Not even Kate knew exactly how involved I'd been in the planning, and I intended to keep it that way. No one needed to know that I'd written up my own schedule and memorized it so we wouldn't get wildly off track.

"You're right," I said, flipping my auburn ponytail off my shoulder. "I guess I don't have anything to worry about."

"Of course you don't," Fern said. "I think this goes to show that you can pull off a wedding without a crazy schedule."

I bristled at the word "crazy," but forced myself to shrug it off as my phone vibrated in my jeans pocket. I walked from my living room to the kitchen as I answered without looking at the name on the screen. I didn't care who was calling as long as it kept me from telling Fern what I really thought about his schedule-less wedding planning.

"Annabelle, thank heavens." Richard's voice sounded high and breathy. "I'm dying."

My best friend and caterer, Richard Gerard, had a tendency to be dramatic, so I took his frequent claims of imminent death with a grain of salt. I dropped my empty Frappuccino bottle into the green recycling bin and hopped up onto the kitchen counter. "Did a waiter show up in a cream shirt instead of white, or did they send you the wrong flatware again?"

"Do I sense a tone of mocking?" Richard asked, his voice instantly sharper.

"Never," I said, hoping he couldn't sense that I was smiling over the phone. "What's wrong?"

"Do you have any idea how hot it is?"

I'd violated one of the cardinal wedding planner rules and forgotten to check the weather report. That didn't mean I hadn't been aware we were in the middle of a heat wave, but at some point, hot was hot. As long as it wasn't scheduled to pour rain on our outdoor ceremony, I was okay with a little heat. "Well, it is mid-July in Washington, DC."

"Which is precisely why it's considered the off-season for weddings. Certainly for outdoor weddings."

"Which is why Leatrice got such a good deal on the venue and all her vendors," I reminded him. "It's also why you were willing to give her the food at cost."

"A benevolent act I'm sincerely regretting."

"I know you don't mean that," I said.

He mumbled something about coercion and self-sacrifice that I couldn't quite make out, and not because we had a bad connection. I knew Richard was only a few blocks away from my Georgetown apartment at the Dumbarton House where Leatrice was getting married. As the caterer for the event, his team was the first into the venue for setup. Normally, I'd be right there with him, but as a bridesmaid I was supposed to be getting hair and makeup done with the bride. A part of me wished I were at Dumbarton House with Richard instead.

We'd chosen the historical home because it was nearby, and it was intimate enough that her small guest count wouldn't be overwhelmed. It also had a lovely garden for the ceremony and a tented patio for the reception. Of course, when we'd toured the venue, it was springtime and in the mid-70s. Summer temperatures in the nation's capital routinely topped ninety degrees with sky-high humidity.

"I take it it's a bit muggy?"

"Muggy?" Richard's voice went up an octave. "I have so many waiters swooning out on the lawn, it looks like they're doing some sort of interpretive dance."

"The temperature should drop by the time we get to the ceremony, and guests are sitting outside."

"Let's just hope I have staff left by that point. I don't know what I'll do if I can't pull off French service."

LAURA DURHAM

I leaned back against my wooden cabinets. "Leatrice is pretty laid back. Worse comes to worst, you can shift to a buffet."

He sucked in his breath sharply. "A buffet?"

"Yes, a buffet," I told him. "They can be done very tastefully."

"If the old bird wanted a buffet, she could have gone to Golden Corral." Richard sniffed. "The menu I planned out is specifically for French service, Annabelle. You know very well I can't just switch it up willy-nilly. It throws off all my quantities."

Richard planned his menus with the same precision I prepared my wedding schedules, so I did appreciate that they couldn't be changed on the fly.

"I know that," I said, "but technically I'm not the wedding planner on this one. You should probably be talking to Fern."

More muttering. "I just hope all the guests aren't as old as the bride. In this heat, we'll have to roll them out on gurneys. Maybe I should serve B12 shooters instead of gazpacho soup sips."

That was a sobering thought, but not an unrealistic one. "I'll call Ace Beverage and have them send a second run of more water and ice. We'll have to keep people hydrated."

"Already done, darling. I'm glad Buster and Mack provided a claw-foot bathtub for our bathtub gin station. Once I fill it with ice, we may have to submerge guests in it to cool them off."

That would make for pretty pictures. "I'll pop over in a few minutes. I'm just waiting for Reese to arrive with the tuxes."

"Has he gotten used to the idea of being Sidney Allen's best man yet?" Richard asked, with amusement in his voice.

"I think so. Sidney Allen did spend a lot of time with Reese while we were in Ireland."

"It's good practice for Reese," Richard said. "Grooms who've been in weddings are always more polished than the ones who are neophytes. We don't want your groom, of all people, to be clueless at his own wedding."

I cleared my throat as my pulse quickened at the mention of

my wedding. I twisted my engagement ring nervously on my finger. "Right."

"Whenever that wedding might be," Richard said, not hiding the sarcasm dripping from his voice. "But don't let me rush you, darling. You just take all the time in the world to pick a date. Not that any of us have busy calendars we need to plan around."

"I'm working on it," I lied. "You know I have to work around wedding season."

Richard let out a long breath. "At least there isn't a set crime season your detective has to worry about. Another perk of being with someone who isn't in the wedding business."

That and there were virtually no single, straight men in the DC wedding industry.

"Considering how long Sidney Allen has been in events, I was surprised he didn't have any other friends." I lowered my voice so Leatrice couldn't hear it through the opening between the two rooms. "Not that Reese wasn't happy to step in."

"I don't see why you'd be shocked. The man's a workaholic and very competitive. Before he met our girl, I don't think he had a personal life."

Richard had known the pint-sized entertainment director for far longer than I had, but I'd also never known Sidney Allen to mention family or friends. Leatrice's quirky fiancé was known for running a company that rented out costumed performers and for micromanaging them on-site while barking orders into a wireless headset. Even though his performers were the most authentic, I rarely used him because I avoided theme weddings like the plague, and he usually amped up the drama factor of any event. Since I routinely worked with Richard and Fern, the drama at my weddings was already high enough. Although we didn't work together often, he'd actually met Leatrice while coordinating a troupe of Venetian performers for one of my weddings.

No one knew his actual age, but I suspected Sidney Allen was younger than Leatrice's eighty-plus years. And while my neighbor was all bones, Sidney Allen was all belly. Each year I'd known him, he'd gotten a little rounder, and each year his pants had shifted higher on his waist. Richard claimed Sidney Allen's pants were actually eating him, and he had suggested an intervention or rescue attempt more than once.

"Your fiancé next to Sidney Allen is going to be quite a picture," Richard said. "One's tall, dark, and handsome and the other—"

"Be nice," I said, my face warming at the thought of Reese being my fiancé and not just my boyfriend. "Not only is he the groom, he's your client."

"Fine," Richard said with a huff. "I just hope he doesn't wear his tuxedo pants hiked up around his armpits."

"I'm sure he'll look fine," I said. "Reese went with him to get fitted."

"Two straight men do not make a right, darling."

I heard a knock on the door, and then Leatrice called out, "Love Muffin!"

I recognized the pastry-themed nicknames Leatrice and Sidney Allen used for each other. "Speak of the devil," I said. "I've got to run."

"Wait," Richard said before I could disconnect. "How is Hermès? Did you tell Fern not to mess with his hair?"

I sighed. Hermès was Richard's dog, although Leatrice babysat him so often, the small dog had been the natural choice for her ring bearer. "I told him."

"The last time Leatrice gave him hair extensions, it took forever for me to get them out," Richard said. "Besides, I just had him groomed."

"The only thing we're doing is putting him in that tiny tuxedo you bought him."

"Good," Richard said. "It should fit him perfectly unless Leatrice has been sneaking him treats since the final fitting."

I tried to suppress the memory of attending a tuxedo fitting for a dog, reminding myself that I was a successful working professional who owned my own business, even if it did involve dogs wearing formal wear. "Talk to you later." I clicked off despite Richard's protests and slid down from the counter.

"You know it's bad luck to see the bride before the wedding," I said as I returned to the living room.

Sidney Allen was indeed standing in my open doorway, but he wasn't alone. A thin man with a full head of silver hair stood next to him, his dark suit a contrast to Sidney Allen's red velvet bathrobe. I looked from Sidney Allen's stricken face to Leatrice's open mouth as she gaped at them.

"I finally found you," the man said, his eyes locked on Leatrice.

CHAPTER 2

"I'm only halfway done," Fern said as Leatrice slipped off the stool and put Hermès on the floor. True to his word, only one half of Leatrice's hair was teased, making her look like she'd been electrocuted on her left side only.

"Is that really you?" Leatrice walked forward and tightened the belt on her Wonder Woman robe, her eyes unblinking as she gaped at the older man next to her fiancé.

The man nodded, working the brim of his hat in his hand. I almost never saw men wear hats anymore, but this old-fashioned gunmetal-gray fedora seemed to fit with his look and his age.

"I've been looking for you for a while," he said, "but don't worry. I haven't told the others I found you."

Hermès scampered up to the strange man, sniffed around his ankles, and proceeded to emit a low growl.

Leatrice let out a breath. "I didn't think it would be you."

"Don't worry," he said. "I'm here for a different reason."

Sidney Allen looked as befuddled as I felt, and I noticed him wringing his hands. What was going on here? I couldn't believe Leatrice had a long-lost love who'd just happened to turn up on her wedding day.

A smile cracked the mystery man's olive skin. "It's been a long time, Leelee."

"Leelee?" Sidney Allen repeated, his voice cracking.

Leatrice blushed. "No one's called me that in an age." She shook her head. "I can't believe it's really Jimmy the Pencil after all these years."

"Jimmy the Pencil?" Kate, Fern, and I said at the same time while Hermès yipped.

Leatrice seemed to remember we were in the room and cleared her throat. "Where are my manners? This is an old friend from another lifetime ago, Jimmy Pinnello." She gestured to us. "Jimmy, these are my dear friends Annabelle, Kate, and Fern, and you already met my honey bun, Sidney Allen."

Honey bun did not look amused. I didn't blame him. The phrase "old friend" seemed suspiciously vague.

Jimmy extended his hand to each of us, lifting mine and Kate's to his lips for a quick kiss. "A pleasure to meet you all."

Kate giggled as she pulled back her hand, and I gave her a look. The name Jimmy made alarm bells go off in the back of my head, but I had too many questions swirling in my brain to say exactly why the name triggered some memory.

"Wait a second." Kate snapped her fingers. "Wasn't your husband named Jimmy?"

So that was why. Leatrice had been a widow for long before we'd ever known her, and I always got the feeling she'd been a widow for longer than she'd been married. My mouth fell open. If this was her supposedly dead husband showing up very *not* dead on her wedding day, I was officially quitting the wedding planning business.

"Leatrice," I said, walking over to her and lowering my voice. "Do you want to tell me what's going on? You do know we're in the middle of a wedding day. *Your* wedding day."

She patted my hand. "Of course, dear. I'm sure Jimmy was dropping by to say hello."

"And Jimmy is...?" I prompted.

"An old friend," Leatrice repeated. "Like I said."

I looked over at the man in question. "So, not your husband?"

"My husband?" Leatrice let out a stream of giggles. "Don't be silly dear. If I had a husband, I couldn't exactly be marrying my honey bun, now could I? No, *my* Jimmy is long gone. "

Sidney Allen relaxed visibly, and I let out a breath. I could scratch bigamy off my list of things to worry about for the wedding.

"Actually, Leelee," Jimmy said, "I was hoping I could have a word with you."

Leatrice bit the corner of her bright-coral mouth, her gaze flitting from him to Sidney Allen. "I'm not so sure now is the best time."

Fern flounced over, still holding his can of hairspray and waved a hand at Jimmy. "As much as I love this wiseguy vibe you've got going on here, we're on a schedule. I still need to work on Annabelle and Kate, and since Annabelle hasn't had a proper haircut in months, it's not going to be quick."

"Hey," I protested.

Fern pretended like I hadn't spoken and continued to address Jimmy. "If you can have your little chat while I work on her hair, be my guest."

"Anything you have to say to Leatrice, you can say to me," Sidney Allen said, finally finding his voice.

"And us," Kate said, touching the edge of her blue pillbox hat. "We're her bridesmaids."

Leatrice's face had flushed pink. "Perhaps Jimmy and I should speak alone."

As I stared at Leatrice, I realized I didn't really know anything about her past. I'd known her since the day I moved to DC over seven years ago, but she was over eighty, so that sliver of time didn't comprise much of her life. I also knew she'd been living in our apartment building for years before I'd arrived, but truth be told, I'd never thought to delve much into her past. Had she always lived in Georgetown? Probably not, but I didn't know where she came from or where she'd grown up. Come to think of it, she never talked about her past.

Now that a bona fide person from her past was standing in front of me, I was struck by just how little I knew about my friend. Even though Leatrice was obsessed with true crime, detective fiction, and rooting out neighbors she was convinced were spies, it had never occurred to me that she'd be connected to someone named Jimmy the Pencil. I had a lot of questions.

"Leatrice?" I plucked Kate's champagne flute from her hand and swigged down the rest of it. "I think you'd better explain what's going on."

Her shoulders drooped. "I'd hoped to take this to my grave."

Kate scooted to the edge of the couch, straightening her hat as it slipped down her forehead. "I told you this was the best wedding day ever."

Directing Sidney Allen to the couch, I motioned for Leatrice to sit next to him. Jimmy took the overstuffed yellow twill chair across from them, while I remained standing. Hermès hopped up and settled himself between Leatrice and Sidney Allen, narrowing his tiny black eyes at Jimmy the Pencil. Fern took up a position behind Leatrice and resumed teasing her hair.

Popping up, Kate grabbed her empty champagne flute from my hand. "I think we could all use a little something to settle our nerves. I know I could, and Annabelle just polished off my drink." She hooked her arm through mine as she passed, pulling me into the kitchen. "Come on, boss. I know Fern stocked your fridge with more bubbly."

"You really want to add alcohol to this situation?" I whispered once we were in the kitchen, and she began pulling cold bottles of champagne from my refrigerator door.

"This is the perfect situation for booze," she said. "You should know. You just polished off my champagne."

"It was my first drop of the day. Not my third glass." I folded my arms over my chest. "You and Fern think every situation is the perfect time for a drink."

She hesitated with a bottle in each hand. "You know, you might be right about that." She motioned with her head to the empty flutes on the counter. "But in this case, it really calls for it. I mean when have we ever had a guy show up in the middle of getting ready and claim to be an 'old friend' of the bride who needs to have a private chat with her?"

"Never," I admitted.

"Exactly. This is either going to be really good or really bad. Either way, we're going to need a drink."

I wasn't sure I agreed with her logic, but I was starting to feel like I'd need more than just the warm dregs of Kate's champagne soon. I picked up as many champagne flutes as I could carry and followed her back out to the living room.

No one had moved, although Leatrice's hair had evened out a bit, and Sidney Allen looked a bit more mollified since Leatrice sat next to him holding his hand.

"What's a wedding day without champagne, right?" Kate asked, setting one of the bottles on the coffee table and peeling the foil off the top of the other one.

I passed out glasses then perched on the arm of the sofa. "So, who wants to tell me what's really going on?"

Leatrice sat forward a bit, and Fern followed suit as he continued to tease the top of her hair.

"First of all," she began, "Jimmy and I are just friends. We always have been."

"We grew up together back in the neighborhood," Jimmy added.

"And that neighborhood would be in . . .?" I prompted.

"Chicago," Leatrice said.

Kate balled up the foil champagne wrapper and dropped it on the table, mouthing the word "Chicago" to me as she cocked an eyebrow.

I shrugged. I hadn't known Leatrice was from Chicago either. She'd never mentioned the city once, as far as I could remember.

"You've never talked about Chicago," Sidney Allen said, taking the words right out of my mouth.

Leatrice squeezed his hand. "I know, cupcake. I left so long ago, and I try not to think about it."

Kate paused as she untwisted the metal cage from the top of the bottle. "Leatrice, did you have to leave Chicago because you're really a fugitive?"

Leatrice let out a tittering laugh. "Aren't you funny? Of course not, dear. At least not in the strict sense of the word."

"Then in what sense are you a fugitive?" I asked, coughing as Fern released a cloud of hairspray over the bride's head.

Leatrice sighed. "I left Chicago to get away from my past." Her gaze darted to Jimmy. "A past that included the wrong kind of people."

I took in Jimmy the Pencil. "Do you mean the . . .?"

"She left the Mob," Jimmy said. "No one leaves the family."

My stomach clenched as I realized I was sitting across from a mobster. Sure, he may be old and seemingly harmless, but I was under no illusions that Mob bosses were nice gentlemen.

"Are you the head of the 'family'?" I asked, rubbing my clammy palms on my jeans.

Leatrice let out another stream of laughter. "Jimmy? Oh, no. He's the accountant."

Now the name Jimmy the Pencil made more sense. My overactive imagination had been coming up with gruesome things you could do with a pencil to earn that nickname.

Kate held the champagne bottle between her legs and started twisting the cork with the hem of her cropped T-shirt. "So you were part of the same family?"

Leatrice looked down to where she clutched Sidney Allen's hand.

"She was the boss's girl," Jimmy finally said.

Fern squeaked and dropped his hairspray. "You were a moll?"

"It was a long time ago," Leatrice said, more to Sidney Allen than to anyone else. "I wasn't much older than twenty."

Sidney Allen stared at her, his mouth hanging open. At least Leatrice's obsession with crime made more sense now, as did why she had her own police scanner. I'd always thought her interest was more detached fascination. It had never occurred to me that she'd ever had firsthand knowledge of crime and criminals.

"So you left at some point?" I asked.

"When Frank was named the new head of the family, I knew I couldn't stay," Leatrice said. "We'd grown up together, and dating him had seemed natural, but the deeper he got, the more I knew the life wasn't for me."

"But Frank didn't want to let her go," Jimmy said. "So I helped her leave and made sure there was no trail for him to find."

Leatrice smiled at him. "I always worried he'd find out how you helped me."

Jimmy gave a brusque shake of his head. "He never suspected. I just did the books after all."

"How is Frank?" Leatrice asked, the corners of her mouth tightening.

"Dead." Jimmy met her eyes. "That's why I'm here. Now that his son's taking over, it's time for me to get out."

"I take it Mob accountants can't just retire?" I asked.

"Not this one," Jimmy said, twisting the brim of his hat. "I know too much. I think this new hothead boss wants to take me out. He's not as reasonable as his father."

I couldn't help glancing at my door. Should I be worried about Mob hitters showing up?

Jimmy leaned his elbows on his knees. "Leelee, you vanished for over sixty years, and Frank never tracked you down. I need you to help me do the same before they find me. You know they'll be on my tail, and they won't be looking to take me alive."

The cork shot out of the champagne bottle with a loud pop, and Jimmy whipped a revolver out of his waistband. We all screamed, Hermès let out a torrent of yips, and Fern dropped to the floor behind the couch.

I put a hand to my hammering heart as Jimmy lowered the gun.

"Sorry about that," he said. "Old habits die hard."

Fern poked his head over the back of the couch and waved to Kate. "Why don't you be a love and pass me that bottle?"

CHAPTER 3

"Are we sure we believe all this?" Kate asked me once I'd pulled her back into my Wedding Belles home office and closed the door.

We'd left a slightly shaken Fern to finish Leatrice's hair with his brush in one hand and the bottle of bubbly in the other. Jimmy the Pencil had put away his gun and had agreed not to produce it again, but Sidney Allen had refused to leave nonetheless. Not that I felt Sidney Allen was especially threatening, but I was glad to have someone aside from a slightly tipsy Fern and an overwhelmed Leatrice to keep an eye on the geriatric goodfella.

"I think it's too crazy not to believe," I said, stepping over pale-pink favor boxes left over from a June wedding. "And it explains a lot of things about Leatrice."

Kate flopped down into my black leather swivel chair. "There are simpler ways to explain an old lady's fondness for Perry Mason than she used to be a Mob boss's girlfriend."

I attempted to pace a small circle over the favors and file folders strewn on the floor. As soon as Leatrice was married, I needed to do a serious cleanup in my office. Actually, I needed to do a serious scouring of my entire apartment, but I pushed that thought out of my mind and tried to focus on the matter at hand. "Have you gotten a good look at Jimmy? He looks like he stepped right out of an old gangster movie."

Kate spun in my chair. "That's what I mean. He's too authentic. Are we sure he isn't one of Sidney Allen's performers?"

I stopped and narrowed my eyes at Kate. "You think the groom arranged for a strange man to burst in and ruin his wedding day?"

Kate shrugged. "Maybe he's getting cold feet."

"Sidney Allen may be an entertainment director, but even he isn't that dramatic. Besides, Leatrice would have to be in on it, and I know for a fact she doesn't have cold feet. As unbelievable as we might find it, she can't wait to get married to her 'love muffin'."

"If I didn't know how gaga Leatrice is for her fiancé, I'd say we were being punked," Kate said. "There isn't a reality show where wedding planners are punked, is there?"

"You're asking me about reality shows? I don't even watch *The Bachelor*."

"Which is a shame. It makes all our couples seem completely normal by comparison."

"Even if there was a crazy reality show that punked weddings, Leatrice would never do that to us."

"I guess you're right," Kate said, eyeing the large, clear plastic bag of custom M&Ms perched on my desk. "It just seems so crazy to think of Leatrice with a past, especially a past that includes her being mixed up with the Mob."

I knew what she meant. I'd only known Leatrice as an old lady with most of her life behind her. I'd never taken the time to think about the long life she'd had before I met her. My cheeks burned with shame that I'd never bothered to ask her where she'd grown up or what life had been like growing up in the forties and fifties. Most of the time, I was annoyed that she was such a busybody and dismissed her obsession with crime as another one of her many quirks. Just like I rolled my eyes at her vintage clothes and oddball outfits. It served me right to be shocked. Leatrice hadn't gone to great lengths to hide her past. Sure, she'd never mentioned it, but none of us had ever asked.

"Why shouldn't she have a past?" I said. "Come to think of it, if anyone would have a crazy past, it probably would be Leatrice. She's in her eighties and still has more energy than either of us; she knows an awful lot about true crime; and she's really good at disguises."

Kate grabbed the customized M&Ms printed with a past couple's names, digging her hand in and then holding it out to me. "But a moll? Do you think she was involved in actual crimes?"

I gratefully took several brightly colored "Andrea" and "Matt" M&Ms and popped them into my mouth. "Leatrice is all about solving crimes and catching bad guys. And this Jimmy the Pencil says she ran from the Mob, which makes me think she didn't want anything to do with being on the wrong side of the law."

"But maybe that's because she's trying to make up for a dodgy past," Kate said, then lowered her voice to a whisper. "You don't think she's killed someone, do you?"

"Of course not. Just because she dated a Mob boss doesn't mean she went around whacking people. Plus, Leatrice said she was really young." I gave Kate a pointed look. "I don't know if any of us would want to be judged by stupid things we did in our teens and twenties."

Kate gave me a side-eye glance. "I may have dated a lot of men, but even I haven't gone out with a Mob boss."

I didn't say that 'Mob boss' might, in fact, be the only category of men she hadn't dated. "We shouldn't judge her before we know the whole story. Besides, I don't know much about molls, but I don't think they were involved in crime. "

Kate shook her head. "I don't know, Annabelle. She's almost killed people before."

"To save us," I reminded her. "And it was always a bad guy."

"I'm just saying, we don't really know Leatrice like we think we did," Kate said through a mouthful of M&Ms. "And if this crazy story is true, how do we know this is her only big secret?"

"You think she's got more in her past than being a former moll and being on the run from a Chicago Mob boss?"

Kate opened her arms wide. "Nothing would surprise me at this point."

The door swung open, and we both jumped. Leatrice stood in the doorway in her Wonder Woman bathrobe, with her dark hair teased into a voluminous Mary Tyler Moore flip. A bird's nest complete with a fake blue bird was attached to the top of her head, and a short veil sprung from the back of it.

"I stand corrected," Kate said.

Leatrice touched a hand to the nest. "Fern said it was very *Sex and the City*. What do you think?"

"I think I'm cutting off Fern's HBO," Kate muttered.

I stuck my head into the hall to look for Fern, but it seemed he had remained in the living room. The pop of another champagne cork confirmed my assumption.

"Fern says he's ready for one of you," Leatrice said, her eyes darting between us. "But before you start, I wanted to tell you what I've decided."

Kate and I exchanged a glance as Leatrice stepped into the room and pulled the door so it was halfway closed.

"I know this is bad timing," Leatrice began, "but I think I have to do it."

"Do what?" I asked, hoping she wasn't saying what I thought she was saying.

"Help. We've known each other since we were kids. Jimmy was always quiet and smart and not like the rest of the boys in the neighborhood. He was Frank's cousin, though, so he worked for the family. Just not in anything illegal."

"Didn't he cook the books?" Kate asked.

Leatrice hesitated. "I suppose he did, but he didn't break kneecaps."

"He carries a gun," I reminded Leatrice.

"Wouldn't you if you were on the run from people you could send to prison?" she asked.

Kate twisted in the swivel chair. "She makes a good point." She swiveled back to Leatrice. "What was it like being a mobster's girl?"

Leatrice's cheeks reddened beneath her rouge. "Not as exciting as you'd think. I didn't know much about Frank's business, although I did go to his club with him. It was the only place you could get a decent cocktail." She giggled. "The dresses were fun, and I always liked makeup."

This was true. She'd been wearing garish lipstick since the day I met her.

Kate shook her head as she gaped openly at my neighbor. "I can't believe you never mentioned this."

"You never asked, dear."

Kate leaned forward. "Have you ever seen anyone get knocked off?"

"Only when I've been with you girls," Leatrice said.

Touché, I thought. When I saw glimpses of Leatrice's sass, I could definitely picture her as a gangster's moll.

"So what happened when you decided to leave?" I asked. "How did Jimmy help you get away?"

Leatrice closed her eyes as if thinking back. "He got documents for me with my new name and gave me enough money to get far away from Chicago. He told me not to tell him where I was going and to keep moving for a while. So I did. After a few years, I figured Frank got tired of looking for me. Knowing him, he found himself a new girl and forgot all about me."

"You changed your name?" Kate asked. "Leatrice isn't your real name?"

Leatrice opened her eyes and smiled. "Oh no. It was Leonora.

I picked Leatrice myself. My mother's favorite silent film actress was Leatrice Joy, so I picked that as a way to remember her."

"So you never saw your family again once you left Chicago?" I asked.

Leatrice's eyes darkened for a moment. "My mother passed when I was twelve. It was only my father and me, and he was too deep in the bottle to notice or care. No, I didn't have much family to speak of, so it wasn't hard to leave it behind."

Watching Leatrice's face, I suspected it had been more difficult than she let on. I wondered if leaving her family and friends behind was one of the reasons she'd become so attached to me and my wedding crew, adopting us as her surrogate family. "Does anyone else know about this?"

She shook her head and cast another glance toward the living room. "No, and I suspect my Honey Bun may be a little upset that I kept this from him."

"You might want to have a heart-to-heart before you walk down the aisle," I said. "I'm an expert in weddings, not marriage, but I don't think secrets are ever a good thing."

Kate took another handful of M&Ms. "Especially when they show up in the form of Jimmy the Pencil."

Leatrice clasped her hands together. "What do you think he'll say when I tell him I want to help Jimmy evade the Mob?"

"I guess it depends," I told her. "What does helping an old friend go on the run from the Mob entail?"

"I think I'd like to know the answer to that question, as well," my boyfriend, Mike Reese, said as he opened the door the rest of the way.

Kate mumbled a curse through a mouthful of M&Ms, and Leatrice spun around, causing the bird's nest to bobble on her head. Reese held an armful of tuxedo bags and wore a scowl that, surprisingly, made him look even more handsome. My gaze was drawn to the single, dark curl that had fallen down on his forehead, and I fought the urge to smooth it back in place.

"Hey, babe," I said, my voice unnaturally peppy. "I was just about to call you."

"Care to explain why Bugsy Siegel is sitting in our living room; Sidney Allen is on the verge of hyperventilating; and Fern is double-fisting champagne?"

"Look on the bright side," Kate said. "No one's dead."

CHAPTER 4

"What do you mean there might be a delay?" Richard shrieked into the other end of the phone.

I held the phone to my head while Fern tugged at my hair as he brushed. Shifting on the stool, I looked over my shoulder to see Reese huddled in conversation with Leatrice and Jimmy. "We're running a little behind; that's all."

"Running behind? You never run behind schedule on the wedding day, Annabelle," Richard said, his voice sounding suspicious. "What's going on? Is the old girl having second thoughts? Is the old boy?" He sucked in a breath. "Is someone dead?"

"No," I said. "Don't be ridiculous."

"I hardly think it's ridiculous that my mind goes to dead bodies," Richard said. "They do seem to turn up a lot at your weddings, darling."

"He's not wrong about that," Fern said, curling the end of my hair around a circular brush and misting it with hairspray.

I tried to shoot him a look as I inhaled the hairspray and coughed. "And who has been with me at almost all of those weddings?"

Richard mumbled something about being dragged kicking and screaming.

"I promise you there's no dead body," I said. "And we're back on track. Leatrice is almost ready; Fern is finishing up my hair; and Kate's getting Sidney Allen ready."

"And Hermès?"

"Free of hair extensions," I said, eyeing the little dog as he paced in front of Leatrice, Jimmy the Pencil, and Reese. The way he glared at the Mob accountant made me rethink his suitability as a guard dog. I suspected he could do some serious ankle damage if the occasion called for it.

"Good. Let's hope you can make up for lost time then," Richard said. "It's sweltering out here, and I can tell you guests won't want to be waiting around for a ceremony to start in this heat."

I gave another quick glance to where Reese sat talking with Leatrice and Jimmy the Pencil. Hopefully, once the two of them explained everything to my cop boyfriend, he'd have an idea of what we should do. As long as those ideas didn't involve a delay in the wedding, everything would be just fine.

"How's the setup going, anyway? I asked, trying not to flinch as Fern yanked my hair back.

"Well, most of my part is done. The chairs are set out for the ceremony; the tables are arranged for cocktail hour; and the ball-room is all set up for dinner. I nixed the tented patio because no one wants to swelter through a three-course dinner, and my salad greens will lose all structural integrity if they sit out in this humidity. I've let my staff go inside to cool off while the floral team sets up the decor."

"Are Buster and Mack already putting out the flowers?" I asked. "Aren't they afraid everything will wilt before we get there?"

"So far they're putting out the furniture and flower stands," Richard said. "Lucky for us you went with a vintage theme.

Some of these settees are going to come in handy when guests start swooning from the heat."

"Very funny," I said. I heard muffled voices in the background, and then Mack's deep voice came on the phone.

"What's this about a delay?" he asked.

I sighed. Bad news traveled fast. Mack was one half of the flower-designing duo from Lush, known among friends as the Mighty Morphin Flower Arrangers. In the DC wedding world, they were famous and infamous. Not only were they notable for creating stunning decor for almost all the society weddings, but they shot the image most people had of wedding florists straight out of the water. Both men were well over six feet tall and three hundred pounds, usually sported head to toe black leather, had a variety of tattoos and piercings, and rode Harleys.

What not everyone knew at first glance, though, was that the burly, bald men with goatees were reformed motorcycle gang members who now belonged to the Road Riders for Jesus. They never cursed, didn't drink, and were total softies. Just hearing the warm rumble of Mack's voice made me feel better.

"No delay," I told him. "We had a little hiccup, but we're getting everything back on track. How's it going over there?"

Richard squawked something in the background, and I had a feeling he hadn't voluntarily given his phone to the imposing florist.

"It's a good thing Leatrice decided to go light on the flowers," Mack said. "This heat is brutal. Buster and I didn't even ride our bikes this morning."

I knew that was saying something since the flower arranging duo went everywhere on their Harleys. I'd even seen them ride up to a church with a box of personal flowers strapped in behind them on the leather seat.

"I know Leatrice appreciates everything you and Buster are doing for her wedding," I said.

"You know we adore her," Mack said with a chuckle. "When she's around, people don't seem to be as startled by us."

I laughed along with him. Even though Buster's and Mack's appearance give some people pause, Leatrice's odd outfits and ever-changing hair color were often just as shocking. I heard more muffled voices in the background, and then Richard came back on the line.

"Snatching the phone from me like that! Of all the nerve." He let out a huff of breath. "He's just lucky he's..."

"Three times your size?" I finished the sentence for him.

"I was going to say he was lucky I was feeling magnanimous," Richard said, his tone frosty. "I suppose I should let you get back to it, although some of us have real work to do and aren't just sitting around primping."

"I'm a bridesmaid," I said. "You know Fern won't let me walk down the aisle with my usual ponytail."

"You've got that right." Fern unleashed a burst of hairspray over my head. "For once in your life you're going to have an actual style." Fern made a disapproving noise in the back of his throat. "The ponytail is the hair world's version of sweatpants, sweetie."

I ignored him and fought the urge to defend sweatpants. "I'll pop by to see how everything is going as soon as I'm finished," I said to Richard. What I didn't say was that by then I hoped Reese had a solution to our little problem.

"If I haven't collapsed from heatstroke by the time you get here," Richard said, before clicking off.

I shook my head as I put my phone in my lap. I wished heat and Richard being dramatic were the only problems I had to deal with today.

"All right," Fern said, patting my shoulders. "You're all done."

I touched a hand gingerly to my updo. "Please tell me there's not a bird's nest on my head."

"Why on earth do you think I would put a bird's nest on your head?" Fern said with a giggle.

I turned and looked pointedly at Leatrice, the nest bobbing back and forth as she talked.

Fern waved a hand at me. "Well, she's the bride. I wouldn't put a bird's nest on just anyone's head."

"Well, that's a relief." I muttered as I slipped off the stool.

"Where is Kate?" Fern swiveled his head around the apartment, as if noticing her absence for the first time.

"I sent her down to get Sidney Allen ready, remember? Of course, that was really just to get the groom out of the way and keep him occupied."

"That's right," Fern said. "No matter. There isn't much I can do with Kate's bob, anyway. Although, I wonder if she'd let me put some butterflies in her hair too?"

"Too?" I felt the top of my head. "I thought you didn't put anything in my hair."

"I said I didn't put a bird's nest in your hair. I never said anything about a few tasteful butterflies."

I didn't even want to see what Fern's idea of "tasteful butterflies" looked like. "This is why I'd rather be the wedding planner than a bridesmaid," I said under my breath as I crossed the room to my fiancé.

Reese looked up at me ,and the corner of his mouth twitched.

"Don't you look like a picture?" Leatrice put her hands to her cheeks and beamed at me.

"I would only do this for you, Leatrice," I said.

Reese stood and walked over to me, placing one hand on my waist. "Are you saying you're not going to do this look for our wedding day?"

My pulse quickened at the mention of our wedding, and heat rushed to my cheeks. "I haven't actually thought about it."

Reese grinned at me. "I'm teasing you, babe."

I tried to smile along with him, but my heart raced. Why did I find it so much easier to plan weddings than to be in them?

"So, did Leatrice and Jimmy tell you everything?" I asked, hoping my quick change of subject wouldn't be noticed.

Reese nodded, his face serious. "You can imagine how

thrilled I am that you and your friends are involved in something illegal during another wedding."

"First of all," I said, "I'd hardly call this illegal, especially
since Jimmy wants to leave a life of crime. Secondly, might I
remind you that these are your friends now?"

"Which is exactly why I've come up with a plan," he said.

"Does it involve arresting anyone?" I asked. "Or calling in
more cops?"

"Not unless Fern tries to put butterflies in my hair."

My cop fiancé was willingly skirting the law and coming up
with a plan to solve a potential wedding disaster? Well, this day
was certainly full of surprises.

CHAPTER 5

"So this is your plan?" I asked as Reese and I walked up the stone steps leading to Dumbarton House. We'd walked the few blocks from our apartment to the nearby venue, since parking in Georgetown was at such a premium, and neither of us wanted to risk moving our cars and losing a space.

"Part of it."

We paused in front of the redbrick Federal-style mansion, with its white columns flanking the portico entrance and its tall windows overlooking the front lawn. The house, which housed the national headquarters of the Colonial Dames of America, had recently gone through a renovation, and I hoped the newly updated air conditioning was up to today's challenge.

I twisted to face my fiancé, dabbing at the moisture on my upper lip, glad I hadn't done my full makeup yet. The stifling heat was making what little I was wearing trickle down my face. "Somehow I thought a plan put together by a DC detective would involve a little more than walking with me to check on the wedding setup."

"As I already explained, I can't be involved in anything illegal."

I waved for him to follow me around the right side of the

house to the garden where voices and the sounds of clattering indicated that event prep was in full swing. "And helping a guy escape from the Mob would be illegal how?"

"First of all, the DC police department doesn't have an organized crime unit, and I'm not Elliot Ness."

"Too bad," I said. "You'd look cute with a Tommy gun."

He shook his head and laughed. "The gangsters used Tommy guns, not the cops. At least in the movies. Like I was saying, there isn't any department protocol on this one, and I can't be involved in anything your nutty neighbor does that's illegal."

"She's your nutty neighbor now, too," I reminded him. We'd only been living together a little over nine months, and although we'd gotten over the initial adjustment, I occasionally had to remind him that he was an official resident of the building and not just a frequent visitor.

"Our nutty neighbor then," he said, sweeping a hand through his hair, the one errant curl falling right back over his forehead. "Since this Jimmy fellow can't use any of his usual contacts to make fake documents, Leatrice is reaching out to her contacts on the internet."

"Boots and Dagger Dan?" I asked as we stepped over a flower bed edging the house's side patio, and I inhaled the scent of mulch and freshly mown grass.

Reese held up both hands. "Don't tell me their names. I do not want to know any more than I need to about our eighty-year-old friend's contacts on the Dark Web."

"She doesn't hang out on the dark web," I explained as we made our way across the stone patio. "She met them when she was trying to be a hacker, remember? You should because you were pretty steamed at me about it."

"Wasn't this before we started dating?"

I nodded. "Back when you were determined to keep me out of criminal investigations."

"That went so well," Reese mumbled. "So Leatrice has kept up with these hackers?"

"I guess. I think they're pretty active on the dark web, which is why they went dark for a while and also why she rarely contacts them. But I guess they can get her the fake documents pretty quickly."

Reese groaned. "That's way more than I needed to know."

"Sorry." I grinned at him, pausing where the patio met the back garden. "But the faster she can get Jimmy the Pencil what he needs to change his identity and go into hiding, the faster we get the old mobster out of our living room."

Reese shoved his hands into the pockets of his khaki pants and rocked back on his heels. "Which is the only reason I agreed to look the other way. That and Jimmy hasn't actually committed a crime in DC."

"So is your plan just looking the other way while Leatrice breaks the law?" I asked. "I mean, I've heard of worse plans, and probably been involved in more than a few myself, but is that it?"

He cocked an eyebrow at me. "No, that isn't it. I have my partner running a few checks on some of the men Jimmy mentioned to see if any might have traveled to the DC area."

My stomach tightened. The thought of more mobsters turning up did not do anything for my nerves. "Hobbes is running the checks? Isn't he coming to the wedding?"

My fiancé's partner in the police department had some sort of long-distance relationship with my go-to cake baker, who lived in Scotland. Since she'd flown over to do Leatrice's cake, I assumed she was bringing Detective Hobbes as her plus one.

Reese shrugged. "I think so, but the wedding doesn't start for a couple of hours, and it doesn't take guys long to get ready."

His mention of getting ready pulled my attention back to the wedding setup. I scanned the walled garden that stretched in front of us, stepping to the side as a waiter rolled a folded-up table by us.

Centered on the high brick wall, the portico that would serve as our ceremony backdrop had a curved alcove flanked by two tall stone urns. The alcove had a curved stone bench and three recessed nooks that held classical sculptures. It was the perfect setting for a ceremony and needed very little adornment, so Buster and Mack had kept it simple, bringing in a collection of plants and trees in pots to accent the alcove and skipping fresh flowers. Not that cut flowers would last long outside anyway.

Vintage couches and armchairs took the place of ceremony chairs and were arranged in groupings facing the alcove, with more plants and trees creating an aisle down the brick path. Off to one side, under the shade of a large tree and next to a small fountain, stood a wooden bar topped with glassware and a white, claw-foot bathtub.

I spotted Buster in black leather pants, a white T-shirt, and a black leather vest adjusting a beige, tufted love seat. He saw me and his face broke into a smile.

"What do you think?" he asked, lumbering over to us.

"It's perfect," I said, standing on tiptoes to give him an air kiss. "Much better than regular folding chairs."

Buster gave Reese a firm handshake then stroked a hand down his dark-brown goatee. "Especially since it's such a small wedding. Chairs would have gotten lost on the lawn."

Neither Leatrice nor Sidney Allen had any family and not many friends, so the guest count was on the intimate side. After learning that Leatrice had left her past behind and changed her identity, I now understood her lack of family.

Buster called Mack over, and the second burly biker florist appeared with a baby on his hip. I wasn't surprised to see the baby girl, who wore a pink sundress and a matching bonnet and giggled happily when she saw us. Buster and Mack had become surrogate fathers to the child when they'd decided to help out the baby's teenaged mother. Prue lived in the apartment over Buster and Mack's Georgetown flower shop and helped them out when she wasn't in class. In return, they watched baby Merry and helped Prue juggle the demands of being a single mother.

I glanced around. "Is Prue here?"

Mack motioned with his head. "She's inside where it's cooler." He looked down at the baby. "I just brought Miss Fussy outside for a little walk."

It was a bit odd to hear Mack's deep voice take on a baby-talk inflection, but I knew both men were dotty over the little girl.

"How's our bride?" Mack asked, his voice reverting back to its normal tone as the baby tugged on his dark-red goatee.

I hesitated, not wanting to lie outright. "It's been a little crazy."

"Wedding day jitters?" Buster asked, giving Merry his finger to squeeze so she wouldn't hang off Mack's facial hair.

I didn't answer, but instead smiled and hoped they would take that as an affirmation.

"I'm surprised to see the best man here." Mack turned his attention to Reese. "Shouldn't you be with the groom?"

"I was escorting Annabelle here so she wouldn't have to walk alone," he said, taking my hand.

"Because Georgetown is so dangerous in broad daylight," I said, rolling my eyes.

Both Buster and Mack ignored my obvious sarcasm and beamed at Reese.

"Isn't that sweet?" Mack said. "Your fiancé can't get enough of you."

I smiled, but inside I was fighting the urge to kick my darling fiancé. As if I needed to be escorted around like a damsel in distress. I squeezed Reese's hand extra hard. "Maybe you should check on Sidney Allen. Kate's been with him for a while."

"You might be right. Are you sure you'll be okay walking back to our place?"

I gave him my most withering look, but he only smiled.

"It's nice to know chivalry isn't completely dead," Mack said.

I was surrounded by helpless romantics. Where was Richard when I needed him?

Buster jerked a thumb behind him. "I'd better get back to work."

"And I need to get this little lady back inside," Mack said, jiggling Merry on his hip.

When both men had walked off, I narrowed my eyes at Reese. "Hilarious."

"Just trying to be convincing," he said. "But, you're right. I do need to check on Sidney Allen. I don't trust Kate with him."

Usually I would agree. I'd stopped assigning Kate to handle the groomsmen on wedding days because she couldn't help flirting with them, and then we ended up with a collection of besotted men. That, and she sometimes gave out other people's phone numbers instead of her own. Sometimes mine. Considering the fact that Sidney Allen could have been her grandfather and had the physique of a Teletubby, I'd thought it was relatively safe. Plus, even though I didn't fully understand it, I knew Sidney Allen was head over heels for Leatrice.

"Let's hope she's used her charm for good and not evil and calmed him down a bit," I said. "He didn't look too thrilled about Jimmy."

"You think?" Reese put his hands on his waist. "I don't know many men who'd be pleased to have a mobster show up on their wedding day and reveal that their bride had once been a Mob boss's moll."

"I beg your pardon?" Richard said, appearing around the corner of the house. "Did you say 'Mob boss'?"

CHAPTER 6

"You seem calm," I told Richard as he stood in front of us with arms folded. Reese and I had taken turns explaining the situation to him, and he hadn't spoken once the entire time.

He looked from one of us to the other, his head tilted and his lips pressed together. Despite the heat, his powder-blue button-down shirt looked crisp, and his perfectly spiked, dark hair had not drooped.

"Do you think we broke him?" Reese whispered.

"Why wouldn't I be calm?" Richard finally said, his shrill voice sounding anything but calm. "I've just learned that the bride, who also happens to be in current possession of my dog, used to be a gangster's moll. On top of that, one of her former Mob associates has popped up unannounced mere hours before she's supposed to walk down the aisle."

"It's a bump," I admitted.

"A bump?" Richard shrieked. "Not only are you telling me we have an extra guest for a seated dinner, which means I'll need to rearrange the seating plan, but now the event design is all wrong."

I glanced at the vintage typewriter set up on a tall stack of old-fashioned leather suitcases, a stack of cream-colored paper next to it so guests could type out messages to the couple. "How is the wedding design wrong?"

"A forties-themed wedding for a former moll?" Richard rapidly tapped one foot. "You know how I hate to be predictable, Annabelle."

"We aren't planning to announce the fact that Leatrice used to date a Mob boss," I said. "I think you're overreacting."

Richard put a hand to his heart. "You know I never overreact. For example, I haven't said a word about the fact that you have flying insects in your hair, which shows remarkable restraint on my part."

Reese glanced at my hair, grinning at me. "He makes a good point."

"See? Your better half understands," Richard said. "I'm not making a big deal out of something small, although why you decided to accessorize with butterflies is beyond me."

I gave an exasperated sigh. "This is all Fern. You know I don't own hair butterflies."

"I should hope not," Richard said, looking at my head and shaking his, then glancing around the garden again. "This is a catastrophe."

"Is he still talking about my hair?" I whispered to Reese.

"Better not to ask," Reese whispered back.

"I've survived worse than this." Richard squared his shoulders. "I just wish I hadn't included miniature cannoli on the dessert buffet."

"Personally, I think it's a good thing that Jimmy the Pencil fits in with the wedding theme," Reese said.

"You're right," I said, snapping my fingers. "We could stick him next to the bathtub gin station, and he'd become part of the decor."

Richard scowled at me. "I thought we agreed no costumed performers."

After a performer in costume had tainted Richard's food at a past wedding, he'd been hostile to the idea of anyone in disguise at his events. If I were being honest, I could do without stilt walkers stepping over me and celebrity lookalikes making me do double takes while I worked. Luckily, I'd convinced Sidney Allen not to use any of his performers for his own wedding since he'd be too busy getting married to coordinate them, and I refused to let him wear his wireless headset on his wedding day.

I took Richard's elbow and walked him toward the back door, hoping to continue our discussion out of the sun. He may be impervious to heat, but sweat was already trickling down my back. "I was joking. If all goes according to plan, Leatrice's friend won't even make an appearance at the wedding."

Reese held open the wooden door, and we all stepped inside the historic house. I felt a blast of cool air as my eyes adjusted to the soft light in the foyer. The high walls were covered with a celadon-green wallpaper featuring rows of large octagons, and the wooden plank floor had been painted to look like black-and-white marble.

"That's a relief." Richard flopped down into one of the bright-green spindle-back chairs lined up near the door. "I'd hate to have PJ put in an awkward situation."

"PJ?" I asked. "You mean the significant other you've been hiding from us?"

Richard huffed out a breath. "Don't be absurd, darling. I'm not hiding him. He's just been very busy."

I gaped at him. "For a year?"

He didn't meet my eyes. "You know these State Department people. Always jetting off to some place or the other."

"State Department?" Reese asked. "I thought he was a bartender or an artist."

"That's what I thought." I gave Richard a pointed look. "At least that's what *someone* told me originally."

Richard shifted in his chair. "I may have told a little fib when we first started dating. Only because I knew what would happen if your batty neighbor got wind of his job."

I thought about Leatrice and her suspicions about people in the government, especially anyone who traveled overseas. "You thought she'd assume he was a spy."

Richard stood up and tugged at his French cuffs. "You know she would, and I didn't want her to start following me or bug my apartment or scare him off with her crazy undercover costumes."

For once, I didn't think he was overreacting. There was a serious possibility Leatrice would have done at least one, if not all, of those things. I'd personally seen her, wearing a blond wig and a trench coat, trailing neighbors she deemed suspicious.

"Not everyone is as understanding as your fiancé." Richard gave Reese a nod, and I knew it was his version of a stamp of approval. "I liked PJ and didn't want to lose him. Or Hermès."

The little Yorkie was officially PJ's dog, although Richard had taken on most of the caretaking duties. Not to mention renaming him from his original moniker, Butterscotch. As much as Richard liked to complain about the dog, I knew he'd be devastated to lose him.

"I get it," I said. I had been lucky Reese had seen past the crazy antics of all my friends, not to mention my own. I reached for his hand and gave it a squeeze.

"I'm sorry, darling." Richard met my eyes. "I know it isn't fair that you haven't met him yet, while I'm practically best friends with your fiancé."

My fiancé twitched next to me. I knew Reese had made a huge effort to befriend Richard, but I wasn't sure if he would have called them "best friends." I made a point not to look at him, for fear his expression would make me laugh.

"It's okay," I said. "At least we get to meet him today."

Richard raised a finger. "If the mobster doesn't show. PJ may not be a spy, but I can't have him involved in any situation that might get him into trouble at work. Although at least now we've been together long enough that he won't be spooked by a few oddball friends."

"Don't worry," Reese said. "It's all under control."

Richard studied his face. "I must say, Detective. Usually you aren't involved in our situations from the beginning. I'm not sure if I find this comforting or disturbing."

"That makes two of us," Reese muttered.

"Why don't you come down to the ballroom and see what we've done with the tables?" Richard said, turning on his heel and heading to the other end of the long foyer.

Reese held me back with one hand.

"What?" I said, looking down at the hand he clasped.

"This PJ fellow…" he began, his voice low.

"Oh, he's definitely a spy," I said. "Richard was right to hide him from Leatrice. Luckily, she'll be too busy today between being a bride and trying to help her Mob friend change his identity to think about it."

Reese laughed and pulled me in for a quick kiss. "That's one of the many things I love about you, babe. You take everything in your stride and always have a solution."

I felt his kiss all the way to the tips of my toes, and I tightened my grip on his hand. "It comes with being a wedding planner. Like I've always said, the military should be sending us overseas to handle delicate diplomatic crises or tricky international conflicts."

He smiled down at me, his hazel eyes deepening to green. "I, for one, am glad they don't. I wouldn't want to be away from you for a single day."

I wrapped my arms around his waist and leaned my cheek against his chest. "Don't worry. Until they assemble the first battalion wedding planner brigade, you're stuck with me."

He rubbed my back as he laughed. "I can't wait to marry you, babe."

My breath caught in my throat, and butterflies fluttered in my stomach. I couldn't do anything but nod and hold him tighter. I planned weddings every day, but the thought of walking down the aisle myself continued to rattle me, which was probably why I'd been dragging my feet about planning my wedding to Reese. It wasn't that I didn't love him and want to marry him. I just had a hard time envisioning myself in the role of the bride when I'd been on the other side of things for so long. Part of me wondered if we should run off to the courthouse instead of bothering with a wedding. But what kind of wedding planner eloped?

"Are you coming or not?" Richard called from the other end of the foyer, his hands on his hips.

"Yep," I said, pulling back from my fiancé and giving him what I hoped was a reassuring smile. My phone vibrated in my pocket and I pulled it out, looking at the screen before answering. "Hey, Kate. How's the groom?"

"Oh, he's fine," Kate said.

I heard Sidney Allen talking in the background, and he sounded upset. "Are you sure? He doesn't sound fine."

"It's not him I'm worried about," Kate said. "It's the other guy."

Reese raised his hands in a question, and I shrugged. I didn't know what my assistant was talking about, but I didn't have a good feeling about it. "What other guy? Jimmy?"

"Annabelle," she said, her voice breaking. "I think he may be dead."

CHAPTER 7

I took a heaving breath as I rested my hands on my knees
and sized up the man crumpled on the floor of Leatrice's
apartment. "This isn't Jimmy."

"I never said it was," Kate reminded me, still holding the
door she'd opened when Reese and I had arrived and pounded
on it.

I took another look at the dark-haired man wearing a black
suit that pulled across his meaty shoulders, grateful for the
hallway light as Leatrice's first-floor apartment didn't get the
natural window light mine did. She'd always told me she kept
her blinds drawn to prevent being spied on by the Russians, but
now I suspected there was a different reason for her paranoia.

I glanced over at my fiancé, who was also busy catching his
breath as he knelt over the body. We'd run the entire way from
Dumbarton House to my apartment building and even though
they were only a few blocks apart, the heat made it feel like a
marathon. I put a hand to my hair as a decorative butterfly
flopped into my face. So much for my wedding day updo.

"He's not carrying any identification," Reese said after he'd
patted down the body, "which is not a great sign. It means he
didn't want to be identified if he got caught."

"So we have an unidentified dead body in the middle of Leatrice's living room?" I said, hearing the tremor in my voice.

"He's not dead." Reese stood up and pulled his phone out of his pants pocket.

Kate sagged against the door. "That's a relief. I didn't mean to give him such a jolt."

"You did this?" I asked while my fiancé walked a few steps away into the kitchen as he talked to his partner and ordered an ambulance.

She produced what looked like a black flashlight. "I got this after the last time we were chased by a homicidal maniac. I figured it might come in handy."

I stepped over the body so I could perch on the arm of Leatrice's floral print couch. I didn't want to touch anything, but I also needed to sit.

"A flashlight?" I looked from her to the man on the floor. "You hit him with a flashlight?"

I gave the living room a cursory glance. None of the fussy furniture or knickknacks in the overly decorated room appeared to be out of place, so I had a hard time believing there had been a struggle. Even the tall stacks of paperback mystery novels on the coffee table hadn't been knocked over.

Kate laughed. "It's not only a flashlight. It's also a stun gun." She held it out. "Want me to show you?"

"No!" Reese and I said at the same time as he rejoined us.

Kate shrugged and dropped the stun gun flashlight back into her pink purse. "Suit yourself."

"So what exactly happened?" Reese asked in his detective voice.

Kate let go of the door and walked further into the room, dropping down into an upholstered armchair with a crocheted doily draped across the top. "I was helping Sidney Allen get ready, like you'd asked. He had a special man's girdle he wanted to try out, so we were trying to fasten him into that when someone knocked on the door."

I tried not to show my surprise at the mention of a man's girdle and avoided glancing over at Reese. Had he known about this? He was Sidney Allen's best man, after all. Had they gone girdle shopping together and he'd never mentioned it?

"I assumed it was Leatrice or you or Fern, so I opened the door." Kate nodded to the unmoving man on the floor. "But it was him."

"Did he identify himself?" Reese asked.

Kate shook her head. "He pushed his way past me into the apartment and started calling out for Jimmy. I told him Jimmy wasn't here and that he had the wrong place, but he told me he knew Jimmy had come here, and he wasn't leaving without him."

"So that's when you stunned him?" I asked.

"I lit him up like a Christmas tree," Kate said, nibbling her bottom lip. "There's a possibility I had the settings too high, but he looked like a big guy, and I didn't want him getting up again."

"Mission accomplished," I told her. "Do Leatrice and Jimmy know about this guy showing up?"

"Not unless Sidney Allen called his bride-to-be and spilled the beans," Kate said, "but I doubt it since I think he's still in shock. I sent him to the bedroom to calm down."

I sighed. "This isn't great."

"Ya think?" Reese dragged a hand through his hair. "Not only are we harboring a mobster on the run, now more wiseguys are looking for him."

My stomach clenched at the thought of more men showing up to our apartment building. We couldn't count on Kate to stun them all.

"Might I remind you that he's not dead?" Kate said. "I think that's a win for all of us."

I didn't like to admit how glad I was we wouldn't be adding another number to our overall wedding body count.

"Luckily, this guy is out for a while, and we can charge him with something to hold him." Reese paced next to the motionless figure. "But I sincerely doubt he's the only one looking for Jimmy. If his people don't hear from him, chances are good they'll send in reinforcements."

Kate popped up. "Then we need to get Leatrice and Jimmy out of here." She looked at me, her eyes wide. "*We* need to get out of here."

I heard the wail of approaching sirens and knew it would be only minutes before the place was swarmed with paramedics and cops.

"If this guy is with the Mob," my fiancé said, "the ambulance and squad cars should keep his buddies away for a while."

I nodded. "We should use this chaos to get Leatrice and Jimmy out. If we don't, Jimmy the Pencil will lead the Mob straight to Leatrice. We can't be sure what they'll do if they discover who she is and that she's successfully hidden from the old boss for years. If his son is as vindictive as Jimmy says, he may want revenge on Leatrice, even though his father is long gone."

"Even if they don't want revenge on her, they probably won't look too kindly on her trying to help Jimmy go on the lam," Reese added.

I heard a commotion in the hall, followed by a loud knocking. Reese opened the door and directed the paramedics to the victim, while briefing them on the situation. They were young, broad-shouldered guys in dark-blue uniforms, and I noticed Kate throw her shoulders back at the sight of them.

I tugged her away from the scene. "Don't even think about it. We're trying to get out of here, not score you a date."

She frowned. "You know I'm an excellent multitasker."

"Not today, you're not. Today you're a bridesmaid whose main duty is to make sure the bride doesn't get bumped off."

Kate put one hand on her hip. "Since when is that something a bridesmaid is in charge of?"

"Since we became bridesmaids," I said.

Reese's slightly doughy partner, Detective Hobbes, followed a pair of uniformed police officers into the apartment as the paramedics began working on Kate's victim. "What have we got?" he asked, his gaze flitting to me and then Kate.

"Attempted burglary," Reese told him. "Assault. He forced his way into the apartment. In response, Kate used her stun gun on him. It was self-defense."

Kate bobbed her head up and down. "I was afraid for my life. Look how big he is."

Hobbes looked down at the thick-necked man, then turned to his partner. "I can file charges after he's released from the hospital."

Reese clapped a hand on the man's back. "Thanks, man. We don't want this to impact the wedding if we can help it."

The detective swept a hand across his thinning hair and appeared to be trying to suppress a smile. "Understood. I'm supposed to meet Alexandra there in a couple of hours."

Hobbes's mention of the cake baker made me think of the setup at Dumbarton House. I needed to call Richard and explain why Reese and I had torn out of there without an explanation. I did not want to deal with him giving me the cold shoulder for the rest of the evening. Or the rest of the summer.

The paramedics raised the gurney and began wheeling the man out of the room. I caught a glimpse of his face for the first time, and it didn't do anything to calm my panic. He had slicked back, jet-black hair and sunken eyes, with a bulbous nose that was turning purple. It looked like it had been broken a few times, and I suspected the most recent time was when Kate stunned him and he'd hit the floor. He looked like he'd stepped right out of a gangster movie.

My fiancé pulled me away by the hand as Hobbes walked around the apartment taking notes. "We need to focus on keeping Leatrice, and the rest of us, safe."

"Which means we get Jimmy, and the potential danger, away from here," I said, feeling myself calm as I focused on the goal.

"I have an idea."

We all turned to see who'd spoken. Sidney Allen stood in the hallway in nothing but a shiny, black, one-piece man girdle that stretched from his upper thighs to mid-chest. His significant girth had been compressed so that it all spilled out the top of the contraption, giving the tiny man an enviable amount of cleavage. The room went silent as even the cops turned to stare at him.

Hobbes looked at Sidney Allen and then at Reese, his pen hovering over his notepad. "I'm going to do us all a favor and leave this out of the report."

CHAPTER 8

"I don't understand," Fern said, his brush still in Hermès's fur.

The tiny dog perched on Leatrice's lap, and the pair sat on the stool by the window. The Yorkie's usually straight black-and-brown fur had been curled into ringlets that made me think of Shirley Temple—if Shirley Temple had also had a shiny, black nose and liked to breathe with her tongue hanging out of her mouth.

Hermès had turned his head as Kate, Sidney Allen, and I burst into the room, and the corkscrew curls were still bouncing around his face. I stifled a groan. Richard was going to have a fit.

"We need to leave," I repeated. "Now."

Leatrice slid off the stool and tucked Hermès under her arm. "What's happened?"

"Yes," Fern said, his gaze shifting to Sidney Allen who'd put on his tuxedo for the wedding but left on the man shaper, so that he now appeared to have a barrel chest and a cinched waist beneath his white dinner jacket. "What on earth is going on there, sweetie?"

Leatrice glanced at her fiancé and did a double take but didn't comment.

"Another one of your old friends showed up downstairs." Kate came in behind me and closed the door, muffling the sounds of the cops still processing the scene on the first floor. "Although this one wasn't so old."

Jimmy stood from where he'd been lounging on my yellow twill couch. "They found me already?"

"Looks like it," I said, hurrying down the hall and snatching the two garment bags hanging from the top of the bathroom door. I hoisted my black nylon tote over my shoulder, glad I'd already packed all my wedding day essentials in it, including my own secret wedding day timeline and copies of all the vendor contracts. "I've got the bridesmaids' dresses. Sidney Allen has your dress, Leatrice."

I poked my head back into the living room and saw Fern sweeping all his supplies into a Prada duffel bag.

"Where are we going?" Leatrice asked, tightening the belt of her Wonder Woman robe. "I thought you said one of Jimmy's guys is downstairs."

"*Was* downstairs," Kate said, pulling the double-duty flashlight out of her purse. "I used my stun gun on him. Now he's on his way to the hospital and then the police station."

Leatrice smiled at her. "Good for you, dear. I had no idea you were packing."

"You know what they say, shoot first, ask questions later." Kate tucked the stun gun back into her purse.

I decided not to debate her interpretation of the phrase at the moment. "The ambulance and police cars should create enough of a distraction for us to get out the back way."

Fern swung his head toward the end of my hallway. "The back way? You mean that rickety old fire escape?"

"It'll be fine," I said with more confidence than I felt. I almost never set foot on the fire escape and hadn't even opened the back door in at least a year. After having my apartment broken into the first time I was involved in a murder investigation, I'd replaced all the door locks with heavy-duty dead bolts. The fire escape was a feature of my building I rarely thought of, but I hoped it would finally come in handy now.

I waved for everyone to follow me down the hall, then stopped when I saw their hesitation. "Would you rather wait for the next Mafia hitter to show up?"

Fern hiked his designer duffel onto his shoulder and bustled forward. "I have no desire to sleep with the fishes, thank you very much." He hooked his arm through Leatrice's and pulled her along with him. "I've never lost a bride to a Mob hit before, and I'm not starting today."

"That's the spirit," Kate said.

I flipped back the dead bolt and opened the door out onto the steel platform that rose four stories over the back alley of my building. I peered down and saw nothing but a garbage dumpster and a dingy paved path leading to the street in two directions. The back of the building didn't smell so great, no doubt thanks to the dumpster combined with the summer heat. Sirens sounded from the front of the building, even though the distance dampened the noise. Reese had stayed behind to give his statement and make sure he didn't spot any other suspicious characters near the building, but I knew we didn't have long until the commotion, and our decoy, would be gone.

"You lead the way and I'll bring up the rear," I told Kate when everyone had assembled outside.

Kate nodded and began backing down the metal stairs. Jimmy moved to go next to Leatrice, but Sidney Allen cut him off. I hoped the two men wouldn't get in a dustup before we could make our escape. The last thing I needed was our groom challenging Jimmy the Pencil to a duel.

"I'll go in front of you, Love Muffin, so I can help you down," Sidney Allen said, patting his fiancée's hand.

Leatrice beamed at him and turned to me. "Can you carry Hermès in your bag? I'm afraid I need both hands to get down."

I took the tiny dog and tucked him into my tote, nestling him between my makeup bag and a three-ring binder. I noticed him trembling and rubbed his head, guessing he felt the same way I did about heights.

When our slow procession had reached the next level down —Kate in her short shorts, Sidney Allen moving stiffly in his white dinner jacket and black tuxedo pants, Leatrice in her superhero bathrobe, Fern doing his take on Mr. Rogers, and Jimmy the Pencil looking every bit the wiseguy—I began backing down with Hermès. The metal creaked, and I clutched the railing tightly, not letting out a breath until I'd reached the bottom.

"Good job, everyone," I said, patting Hermès on the head again and noticing that Sidney Allen looked a little green around the gills. "Now follow me."

I realized just what an odd group we made after we wound our way through the back alley and came out onto the street. Maybe in some areas of DC a tiny old lady in a superhero robe with a bird's nest on her head wouldn't be noticeable, but chic Georgetown was not one of those places. I only hoped anyone looking for Jimmy would be so distracted by Leatrice's getup or Kate's Daisy Dukes that they'd miss him.

I shot a few furtive looks behind me as we hurried through the historic neighborhood lined with brick row houses and shaded with tall trees. Although cars were definitely slowing down to stare at us, none of the occupants looked more than curious or amused.

"How much longer?" Fern said, his voice breathy. "This humidity is ruining all of my hard work. Just look at poor Hermès."

I glanced down and saw that the Yorkie's curls had frizzed so that he looked more like Little Orphan Annie than Shirley Temple. "Almost there."

"Are we going to a safe house?" Leatrice asked as Sidney Allen held her by the elbow and waddled along beside her, his gait jerky from the obviously too-tight man girdle. His face was flushed red, and I hoped he wouldn't pass out on me.

"Sort of," I said. "It should be the safest place for us thanks to Sidney Allen's quick thinking."

Leatrice smiled up at her honey bun, and his puffed-out chest became even more so.

I led the way down Q Street and then up the steps of the house, throwing open the front door as everyone filed in.

Leatrice swiveled her head to take in the high-ceilinged foyer. "It's our wedding venue."

"Exactly," I said. "Not only are Buster and Mack here, your fiancé made a few calls so that Jimmy will be easier to hide at the wedding."

A short, stocky man in a black suit with a thick white pinstripe and a matching fedora pulled down low over his eyes walked in from the door at the end of the hall. A slender woman in a lavender flapper dress followed, the glittering bugle beads covering the dress clicking against each other as she waved her long white cigarette holder at us. "Hey, dolls."

Richard stepped out of the parlor directly off the foyer, and his gaze scanned our motley group. He lingered for a moment on Hermès, his face twitching. Folding his arms across his chest, he narrowed his eyes at me. "Boy, do I have a bone to pick with you, Annabelle."

CHAPTER 9

"I thought you promised me there would be no costumed performers," Richard said, dodging a cigarette girl with a tray hanging from her neck.

"I'm sorry," I said, as Richard led us into a room adjoining the foyer. "It's part of the plan."

Richard swung his gaze to Sidney Allen. "I suppose this was all your idea in an attempt to sneak your performers into the wedding day somehow."

Sidney Allen walked jerkily to the white plaster fireplace, his footfall echoing off the wooden plank floor, and leaned one hand against the mantle as he caught his breath. "I beg your pardon. I'm only doing this to help my cupcake."

"How does this help Leatrice?" Richard asked.

I darted a glance out the front window. "Sidney Allen thought that Jimmy the Pencil wouldn't stick out so much if there were a bunch of people dressed like they'd stepped out of the forties."

Richard's gaze swiveled to the stocky man in the dark suit and fedora, and his pupils widened slightly. "I see." He gave the aged gangster a simpering smile before taking me by the elbow and propelling me back into the foyer. "Are you out of your mind?"

I pulled my arm from his. "What? As far as harebrained schemes go, I thought this was one of the better ones. It's better than the time you put on a tasting to smoke out a killer."

"That was your idea!"

A passing flapper jumped in surprise, and Richard mumbled an apology.

"I know," I said, "but this one is better. We're only doing it to keep Jimmy hidden and Leatrice from being discovered. It's more of a diversion than anything."

Richard sniffed, looking slightly mollified. "I suppose I don't want the bride being tracked down by the Mafia on her wedding day."

"You're such a softie," I said, winking at him.

"Yes, well. Do you care to explain this fiasco?" Richard waved a hand at Hermès, who was still tucked in my bag, his frizzy head straining to reach Richard's flapping fingers.

I rubbed the dog's head. "Humidity?"

Richard lowered his voice to a whisper as he let the Yorkie lick his fingers. "He looks R-I-D-I-C-U-L-O-U-S."

"Did you just spell in front of the dog?"

Richard arched an eyebrow at me as he lifted Hermès out of my bag. "He's very clever, Annabelle. I don't want to hurt his feelings."

"You make comments about my hair and clothes all the time," I said. "You aren't worried about hurting my feelings?"

He gave my jeans and T-shirt a quick once-over. "I'm hoping one day you'll listen to me, darling. You know when I talk about fashion travesties, it's expressly for your benefit. I already know how to accessorize." He started to go back into the room and looked back. "So does the dog."

I followed him, telling myself to forget being compared to a dog and coming up short. I needed to focus on the current wedding day problem.

Leatrice stood at the fireplace with her arms wrapped around her fiancé's unnaturally small waist, the bird's nest on her head reaching his chin. "If you should be upset at anyone, dear, it should be me," she told Richard. "My Sweetie Pie is only trying to help me return a favor for an old friend."

"Anything for my Sugar Muffin," Sidney Allen said, peering down at her.

Richard flinched at the pet names, sighing as he spun to face me. "How am I going to feed all these people, Annabelle? I don't have enough vendor meals for two dozen extra gangsters, molls, and showgirls."

Kate sank down into an ice-blue damask chair by the doorway. "I think vendor meals are the least of our problems."

"You can say that again." Fern dropped his duffel and began digging through it. "I have less than a hour to repair all this hair and do makeup. Annabelle, your butterflies are looking less than fluttery."

I touched a hand to my drooping hair. "I know the feeling."

Richard strode across the room, Hermès tucked under one arm, and hoisted Kate up from the chair. "No sitting on the historical furnishings," he reminded her. "I, for one, do not want to be on the hook for damages."

Kate swept her gaze around the room, which was sparsely furnished with period pieces that looked delicate and less than cozy. "The Federal period was so uncomfortable."

"We shouldn't stay here," I said, motioning to the tall, bare windows that let light stream into the room. "Anyone can see straight inside. Anyway, we should put Jimmy with the performers."

Jimmy shifted from one boot to the other. "I need to perform?"

"Absolutely not," Sidney Allen said. "My performers train for months to comport themselves properly on site. You aren't close to being ready."

Jimmy nodded but seemed befuddled. I wondered if all this

was confusing for him. After all, if he was Leatrice's age or older, that would put him in his eighties.

"Don't worry about it," I told him. "Just be yourself. You're the real deal."

"I should go check on my team," Sidney Allen said, motioning to Jimmy. "Come with me, and I'll get you in place."

"And I need to get the bride into her gown," Fern said, linking his arm through Leatrice's. "And repair the nest."

Fern and Leatrice swished out of the room, her Wonder Woman robe flapping behind her. It took Sidney Allen longer to lurch his way across the room and out the door with Jimmy.

Richard waited until he'd gone to spin around and glare at Kate. "Is that your doing?"

"Is what my doing?" Kate asked, flipping her fingers through her hair.

Richard tapped one foot on the hardwood floor. "The man looks like he's been shoved into a corset. I know you didn't put a groom in Spanx."

"Don't be silly," Kate said. "They don't make Spanx that can hold in *that* much."

I shuddered as I remembered the glossy, black foundation garment that looked like a cross between an industrial-strength girdle and a dominatrix outfit. "That thing did look a lot like a corset."

Richard pivoted to me. "Say it wasn't you, Annabelle."

"Where would I get something like that?" I said. "You know my idea of lingerie is one of Reese's oversized T-shirts."

"Too much information." Richard returned his gaze to my assistant. "Annabelle's right. You're the only one in our group who's familiar with kinky underwear."

"I beg your pardon." Kate tried to look offended, but then shrugged. "Fine, I know my way around a bustier, but what Sidney Allen has on is more along the lines of industrial-strength shapewear. And it was all his idea. I only helped with the fastening." She let out a breath. "Trust me when I say it's a two-person job."

"Well, he looks like he's about to keel over," Richard said. "The last thing we need is the groom dropping during the ceremony."

Kate shuddered. "Agreed. I've had enough bodies dropping for today."

"Excuse me?" Richard's eyes grew wide. "To what other bodies are you referring?"

I gave Kate a look. I'd hoped to keep the second mobster a secret for a little while longer. "The reason we all came running over here is because one of Jimmy's colleagues showed up at Leatrice's apartment looking for him."

Richard took a step back. "Colleague? You mean another member of the Mafioso?"

"Don't worry," Kate said. "I took him out with my stun gun."

Richard's mouth opened and closed. "Your stun gun?"

Kate whipped it out of her purse. "See? It's a flashlight and a stun gun." She flipped on the beam of light then pressed a button and the cylinder hummed. "Kills two birds *and* a stone."

"With one stone," I said, correcting her halfheartedly, knowing she'd mangle the expression again regardless.

Richard raised his palms to silence us. "Where's the other mobster now? Please don't tell me he's tied up in a closet somewhere or rolled up in Leatrice's carpet."

Kate snapped her fingers. "Good thinking. We should have stuck him in a closet. That would have saved us all the hassle of the paramedics and police."

"He's probably at the hospital by now," I said. "Then on his way to be booked for B & E. Reese and his partner were handling it while we got Leatrice and Jimmy out of the building."

Richard pressed a hand to his heart. "So you're telling me that the Mob is after this Jimmy the Pencil, and they've already tracked him down to your apartment building? And that now you've led them here?"

"They don't know we're here," I said. "We went down the fire escape and through the back alleys."

Richard walked over to one of the high windows, scanning the front lawn and the stairs leading down to the street. "You think a thousand-year-old woman in a superhero bathrobe with a bird on her head, running around with a man in a corset, Daisy Duke, and Al Capone wasn't noticed?"

"You know she's not that old," I told him.

"If the Mob is prowling the streets of Georgetown for Jimmy, Leatrice's getup would have distracted them so much they probably wouldn't even notice him," Kate said.

I nodded in agreement. "The wedding will be over in six hours anyway. We just have to keep him hidden until then."

"Okay, Miss Problem Solver. What happens to him after the wedding?" Richard asked. "Does he go on the honeymoon with the nauseating couple?"

"Leatrice has her hacker friends working on fake documents for him so he can disappear," I said. "Fern was there when she contacted them. He said it was a little scary how good she is with all that stuff."

I was reminded again that Leatrice was not really named Leatrice at all, and that she'd successfully changed her own identity and lived under an assumed name for most of her life. After all this was over, Leatrice and I were going to have a long talk about how she pulled it off.

"I'm surprised Reese is okay with this plan," Richard said, his gaze settling on me.

"He's not involved with that part of the plan, but he's fully on board with getting Jimmy the Pencil out of our hair."

"You mean your cop fiancé doesn't want a career criminal hanging out in his apartment?" Richard drawled. "Imagine that."

"Speaking of hunky Detective Reese," Kate said, tapping her

fingers on her chin as she stared out the window, "is there any reason he would be chasing Sidney Allen around the front yard?"

I leaned up against the window and watched Sidney Allen careening across the small lawn, his torso completely rigid and wobbling back and forth as he attempted to run without moving his upper body. His hands flapped at his side, presumably to keep balance.

Richard made no effort to hide his gaping jaw as Hermès yipped in excitement. "He's not chasing Sidney Allen."

We all watched as Reese overtook the overly cinched Sidney Allen and kept running.

"You're right," I said. "They're both chasing Jimmy the Pencil."

CHAPTER 10

"That wasn't much of a chase," Kate complained as Reese escorted Jimmy the Pencil back into the house.

"I don't know about that," I said, inspecting the state of Sidney Allen as he wheezed inside the foyer, sweat running down his round face.

"We were in the back garden," Sidney Allen said between attempts to catch his breath. "I took him to the paved patio to the side so I could show him where we had the cigar station. That's when he started running."

I studied Jimmy, who was also breathing heavy, his elbow held securely by my fiancé. His suit was rumpled, and bits of grass clung to his pants from being brought down by Reese. The scent of freshly mown grass mingled with his cologne. "Why did you run? Did you see someone you knew?"

Jimmy rubbed his face and then dragged a hand through his silver hair. "I thought I did. So many people here remind me of fellas from back in the day."

"I guess having all the actors dressed up did a good job of confusing things," I said. It hadn't occurred to me that in trying to confuse any Mob hit men, we'd also flustered the elderly Mob accountant.

"Good thing I was walking up the stairs when I spotted Jimmy making his escape and Sidney Allen in hot pursuit." Reese patted the groom on the back. "Not that my friend here didn't have it well in hand."

I knew Reese was being gracious and trying to make Sidney Allen feel better. The old mobster had left the girdled entertainment diva in the proverbial dust.

"It's surprisingly difficult to run in this tuxedo," Sidney Allen said, straightening his white dinner jacket.

Richard opened his mouth to make a comment, and I elbowed him.

"What?" Richard rubbed his side where I'd made contact. "I was only going to say that he should open his top jacket button the next time."

"Sure you were," I said under my breath and watched Richard's face redden.

The front door opened, and four willowy women in black cocktail dresses entered carrying instrument cases. I directed them through the house to the back garden, making a mental check mark that the string quartet had arrived. I pulled my phone from my pocket and looked at the time.

"Right on schedule," I said.

Kate smirked at me. "I knew you had a schedule. You couldn't resist, could you?"

"Every wedding day needs a schedule," I said. "There's no such thing as a wedding running smoothly on its own."

"I'm with you," Kate said, looping her arm through mine. "I miss checking things off."

Reese cleared his throat. "Why don't I handle this guy while the rest of you handle the wedding?"

I nodded as butterflies fluttered in my stomach. "We don't have long until guests arrive."

"I know," Reese said, giving me a crooked smile. "I can see the panic on your face."

I wanted to tell him that I never panicked, but he knew me

too well. We were closing in on start time for a ceremony I was not only supposed to run, but was a part of, and I was still in jeans and hadn't done makeup or repaired my hair. I took Reese's free hand and squeezed it. "This is why I love you."

He wiggled an eyebrow at me. "I hope it's not the only reason."

My cheeks warmed and I realized everyone in the foyer was watching me, even Jimmy the Pencil. "You heard the detective. He's got Jimmy, so the rest of us need to finish getting ready."

Richard looked down at Hermès as he headed off. "You and I need to do something about this hair."

Kate patted my arm. "I think it's time we transformed into TWA stewardesses."

I cast a final, longing look at Reese as Kate pulled me away and down the stairs to the basement. I'd much rather keep watch over a member of a dangerous crime family who was also a potential flight risk than get into my bridesmaid's dress. From Reese's wicked grin, he knew it.

We descended the stairs and passed through some of the Colonial Dames offices before reaching the ballroom with butter-yellow walls, brass chandeliers and wall sconces, and arched French doors that opened out onto the lower tented patio. Round tables had been set throughout the room—along with a single long oval head table—and draped with white organza linens. Clear ladder-backed reception chairs ringed the tables, while sleek arrangements of white calla lilies and massive green palm fronds rose from the middle, giving the room a slight supper club vibe. Even though we'd kept the wedding simple, Buster and Mack hadn't been able to resist dramatic, yet simple, florals. Nor had Kate and I resisted menu cards printed in a chic art deco font. I smiled when I saw that each menu card had been tucked into a white linen napkin folded to look like a tuxedo jacket.

"Look!" Kate pointed to one perfectly folded napkin. "It looks just like Sidney Allen's dinner jacket."

"Don't you love it?" Mack asked, weaving his way through the tables toward us with baby Merry strapped to his chest in a front-facing baby carrier. "Prue has been folding them all day."

I looked over to where the teenager sat with a small stack of napkins and waved. Her ash-brown hair was swept up into a ponytail, and the freckles across her nose made her seem even younger than her eighteen years. "Hey, Prue! This looks amazing."

Her cheeks flushed. "Richard taught me. He told me if I was going to hang around weddings, I might as well learn something useful and not be a bump on a log."

"That sounds like Richard," Kate muttered.

"Be careful he doesn't start putting you to work at all his events," I said, although I didn't think it was a bad idea that the single mother was learning practical skills from both a caterer and a floral team.

I noticed that the baby was asleep and lowered my voice to a whisper. "It looks like everything is almost set."

Mack waved a hand and glanced down at the tiny head lolling to one side. "Don't worry about your talking waking her up. She's out like a light, and she's used to noise."

That made sense considering neither Buster nor Mack could be deemed quiet. Between the chains on their clothes that jingled, the roar of their Harleys, and their naturally booming voices, Merry must have gotten used to sleeping through anything.

"Do we have guests already, or did Sidney Allen send a team of impersonators that I didn't know about?" Buster asked, walking in from the patio.

"The second one," Kate said, "but only because we need them as a distraction so the real mobster won't look out of place as we hide him from the hit men who're after him."

Buster and Mack froze, and Prue's eyebrows shot sky high.

"It's a long story," I said, "but that's the gist of it. Oh, and back in the day, Leatrice used to be a Mob boss's moll."

"And she changed her name and went on the run," Kate added.

"Now her old friend, Jimmy the Pencil, wants to escape the Mob and needs her help," I said. "So we're hiding him from the other members of the crime family."

"I already took out one of the hit men who's after him." Kate hiked her purse higher onto her shoulder and turned to me. "I think that's everything, right, Annabelle?"

I thought for a second. "Those are the pertinent facts."

Mack pivoted to Buster and let out a tortured sigh. "I've always said we miss things when we do setup at the venue. All the juicy stuff happens during getting ready."

"Can we do anything to help?" Buster asked.

"If you see anyone trying to garrote a gray-haired man, stop them," Kate said.

"How about we stop any garrotting?" Mack asked.

"But be subtle," Kate said. "And don't kill anyone. We're really trying to keep this wedding dead body free."

Buster raised his eyebrows, and the motorcycle goggles on his bald forehead shot up. "We could never kill."

"Right," Kate said. "'Thou shall not kill.' That's one of the biggies."

"Not to say we wouldn't apply a choke hold if the occasion called for it," Mack added.

I heard the faint sounds of a string quartet warming up, and my stomach did a somersault. "Now Kate and I need to get changed before I become the first bridesmaid in history to walk down the aisle in jeans."

I turned to head for the ladies room and almost ran into a tall woman with long, brown hair and a flowing, pink maxi dress slit up to her upper thigh. Luckily, her wide-brimmed hat was too high to hit me in the face.

"Annabelle! Kate! I've been looking for you two. Did you see the cake?"

It took me a moment to realize the glamorous woman who

looked nothing like a cake baker was, in fact, our cake designer Alexandra. I breathed in her seductive scent of expensive perfume and sugar as she leaned in to hug me.

"Not yet," I said. "It's been a crazy day, and we still need to get dressed for the ceremony."

She waved a hand, and her jeweled rings flashed at me. "Of course. Don't let me stop you. It's been a wild day all around, hasn't it?"

I paused, twisting around until I spotted the cake table with a simple two-layer wedding cake on a silver cake stand. Sugar calla lilies topped it, and sugar flower petals surrounded the base. "No problems with the cake, I hope."

"Of course not," her exotic voice trilled with laughter. "The cake is darling, and I made sure to put extra sugar petals around for you to nibble on later."

She knew me well as I often used her sugary décor to give me a much-needed boost at the end of a wedding.

"It's my date," she continued. "Apparently he might be late. Trouble at work."

That stopped me cold. "Do you mean Detective Hobbes?"

She nodded, flipping her stick-straight hair off one shoulder. "The criminal they were guarding at the hospital escaped."

The butterflies in my stomach turned to lead. This was not good.

CHAPTER 11

"This is intolerable," Richard said, coming into the Dumbarton House foyer from the garden and leaning against the door after he closed it. A burst of stifling heat followed him, quickly dissipated by the air conditioning.

"I know we're running a couple of minutes behind schedule," I said, trying not to move as Fern readjusted the decorative hair butterflies around the light-blue pillbox hat he'd perched on top of my head. "I don't think this wedding should go against my punctuality record considering all the extenuating circumstances."

"I'll second that," Fern said, his voice garbled as he held a row of bobby pins between his lips. "I've rarely had to do the entire bridal party's hair twice. Including the dog ring bearer."

I shifted my eyes down to look at Hermès scampering around our feet in his tiny tuxedo. Fern had used a significant amount of hair product to get the dog's fur into bouncy ringlets again, and I could smell the scent of Aveda wafting off him. Fern gave my hair a final pat and spritz of hairspray before stepping away.

"It's not your record I'm concerned about." Richard smoothed his tan suit jacket and flicked a glance at Fern, who had changed into a long black priest's cassock with a gold sash and a shoulder cape topped with a massive gold cross. "It's the men's bald heads. The sun is so hot, they're swiping my linen cocktail napkins from the bar and draping them over their cue balls."

"What?" Kate put a hand over her mouth to stifle a laugh as she went to the tall windowpanes on either side of the door.

I followed her lead, peering out the other side window to see that several of the guests lounging on the vintage furniture wore linen hemstitched cocktail napkins as hats. I noticed that the women had taken the folding fans we'd tucked into baskets at the back of the ceremony area and were fanning themselves vigorously. I spotted Alexandra and her hat sitting near the front.

Richard let out a tortured sigh. "My Irish linen hemstitch are covered in head sweat. If only this was a Jewish wedding, and we had yarmulkes to offer the baldies."

"If I remember correctly, this isn't the first time this has happened to you," I said, turning away from the window and toward Richard.

"It's the first time it's happened with my imported Irish linen." Richard pursed his lips. "I'm going to have to hand launder them."

"Maybe instead of cigarette girls, we should have sunscreen girls," Kate said. "Or those misters like they have at the zoo, but instead of water, they mist out sunscreen."

"Now that's a clever idea, isn't it, Sweetie Pie?" Leatrice said from where she stood at the back of the processional line. She'd changed out of her superhero bathrobe and into her wedding dress, a drop-waist ivory gown made of embroidered silk and organza that reached her ankles. Fern had done an admirable job of finding a dress that hid the fact that Leatrice had no discernable curves and an overabundance of loose skin. The illusion sleeves reached her wrists, covering up most of her age spots, and the sheer bodice came up to her neck.

Sweetie Pie gave her a weak smile. Even though he would be walking out before she did, Sidney Allen had refused to leave Leatrice's side since we'd found out the man who'd forced his way into her apartment had escaped police custody.

"The good news is the sun is going down, so we're already past the hottest part of the day," I said.

"Tell that to the napkin heads," Richard grumbled.

I looked over my shoulder and did a mental rundown of the processional lineup. We were still missing a few key people, but I tried to suppress my desire to panic. Going over the order in my head would calm me down. First would be the officiant, Fern, followed by Sidney Allen and his best man, Reese. Then Kate and I would walk, followed by Richard with Hermès ,the ring bearer, and Prue wheeling baby Merry in an old-fashioned pram adorned with flowers. Finally, Buster and Mack would escort Leatrice down the aisle, one on each arm. It would be charming and emotional, if only half the people weren't MIA.

"We're here," Mack said, as he appeared from the staircase leading downstairs. "And we have the flowers."

I let out a sigh of relief as I eyed the long white box in his arms.

"And I have the flower girl," Buster said, walking behind holding Merry in his arms. The little girl wore a white dress and waved a floral head wreath that I knew would never actually sit on her head.

"You look great, Leatrice," Prue said as she came up the stairs in a pretty yellow sundress that made her look even younger than she was.

Leatrice beamed and patted her hand. "Aren't you a dear?"

Mack set down the box and began doling out bouquets. Leatrice squealed with delight when she saw her ivory teardrop bouquet with sprigs of blue hyacinth tucked between the roses and lilies.

I picked up the boutonnieres, took two, and handed the clear box to Kate. Years of practice had made both of us experts at pinning on flowers, and we quickly pinned Richard, Hermès, and Sidney Allen. I hesitated when I reached Buster and Mack.

"I don't think I can get the pin through your leather," I told them.

Mack winked at me as he dug around for a smaller flower box. "I made two with magnets." He pulled out the blue hyacinth boutonnieres and showed me the magnet backs before snapping one on his leather jacket and one on Buster's.

Part of me had hoped they'd lose the black leather for the wedding, but I noticed that they'd changed into their "good" leather, so I decided that was a win.

"I don't suppose you know where the best man gallivanted off to?" Richard asked, his pointed gaze fixed on me.

"I'm guessing he's doing something related to the guy who slipped out of police custody," I said. "The last I saw he was talking to Hobbes and arranging for extra security for the wedding."

"First a troupe of actors pretending to be wiseguys and now a security team?" Richard groaned. "What happened to the low-key, intimate wedding I was promised? 'You won't even feel like you're working,' you said. 'It will be so simple, you can do it with your hands tied behind your back,' I believe were your exact words."

"Being tied up is still an option," Kate said under her breath, looking away quickly when Richard shot daggers at her.

"Stick to beverage service, darling," Richard drawled, letting his gaze linger on the robin's-egg-blue suits that did make us look like stewardesses straight out of the fifties.

I took the bouquet of white flowers Mack handed me. "Be nice, everyone. This is a wedding, after all. We're here to celebrate Leatrice and Sidney Allen."

Fern unfurled a handkerchief from underneath his shoulder cape and blew his nose. "I can't believe it's finally here. I just hope I don't lose it during the ceremony."

"Me too," I said. "Especially since you're performing it."

Fern's head snapped up. "Good heavens, that's right. I was so busy beautifying everyone, I almost forgot that part."

"You do have the ceremony script, right?" I asked, realizing for the first time that he held no papers or portfolio from which to read.

"Don't be silly." He waved the handkerchief at me then tapped his temple. "It's all up here."

"Now can we admit this wedding is a disaster?" Richard muttered as he sidled up to me.

"Everything is going to be fine," I said, more to reassure myself than to convince him. "Remember, none of the guests know that any of the changes aren't what we intended all along. That, and no one is better at faking things than Fern."

The hairstylist shoved the handkerchief into his pocket and took Leatrice's hand. "What do you think about incorporating some Hindu elements into the ceremony?"

"I'm pretty sure they'd know *that* wasn't what we intended," Richard said.

Before I could tell Fern to stick to the nondenominational ceremony that didn't require a small pyre, the front door to the house opened, and my fiancé stepped inside in his tuxedo ,followed by a man in a black suit who looked remarkably like him.

"Daniel!" Kate said, her face lighting up at the sight of Reese's older brother.

"I guess this is the extra security," Richard said, nodding appreciatively at the broad-shouldered man with dark hair shot through with gray at the temples.

Daniel Reese had been a cop and now ran his own private security firm. We'd met him when he'd been called in to provide extra muscle for one of my weddings, and he now made an appearance whenever my fiancé needed help that fell outside the purview of the DC police department. He was almost as handsome as Reese, and seemed to have a special ability to make Kate forget her "never get attached" policy.

"Sorry I'm late," Reese came up and put an arm around me.

I ran a hand down the smooth fabric of the black tux, thinking how good he looked all dressed up. "You're forgiven." I could see the worry in his eyes, even as he smiled at me. "I take it they haven't found the guy yet."

He shook his head. "They did get a positive ID on him, though. Turns out he's Jimmy the Pencil's nephew."

"His own nephew was sent to kill him?" I asked, my voice louder than I'd intended.

Reese pulled me a few feet away as everyone swung their heads toward me. "I need to talk to Jimmy again. His nephew arrived in DC this morning with another man. I need to know if the other man is also a hit man. Where's Jimmy now?"

"He should be outside waiting for the ceremony. Last time I checked he was on the ivory settee in the front."

Reese took a few long steps to the window by the door. "He's not there now." He swiveled his head from side to side. "Found him. He's with the band."

"The band?" I joined him at the window. "We got a swing ensemble for dancing, but they aren't supposed to play until later."

Sure enough, Jimmy the Pencil stood next to a standing bass and a singer in a flapper dress. He held a microphone and seemed to be crooning away.

"Is that Sinatra?" Fern asked, cocking his head to one side.

"What else?" Reese asked.

"Do you think he could sing 'It Had To Be You' for me to walk down to?" Leatrice called from the back of the line.

I resisted the urge to run out the front door and never look back. "So much for him keeping a low profile."

CHAPTER 12

"**G**reat ceremony, doll," one of the cigarette girls said to me as she leaned up against the brick wall of the house. "I've never seen one that fast before."

I smiled at her as I held the door open so the rest of the wedding party could duck inside. It had been all of six minutes since we'd processed from the house's foyer to the garden. I was pretty sure the processional had taken longer than the actual ceremony.

The last few notes of Mendelssohn's "Wedding March" died out as I closed the door behind me, grateful to be back in the air conditioning, but startled that we were back in the foyer so soon.

I saw Leatrice still clutching Sidney Allen's hand and looking a bit dazed. Sidney Allen looked as if he might pass out from the heat and his corset. I steered them both toward green cane-back chairs so they could sit.

"That's it," I plastered on a fake smile as I looked around and tried to find Fern. "You and Sidney Allen both said 'I Do,' right?"

Sidney Allen exchanged a glance with his bride. "I think so. It was a bit of a whirlwind."

That was putting it mildly. We'd indeed processed down the

aisle to Jimmy the Pencil singing "It Had To Be You," and then Fern had welcomed everyone before launching into vows that sounded only vaguely like the traditional ones found in *The Book of Common Prayer*. I'd been preoccupied by my concern that Jimmy might wander off or that one of his Mob buddies might wander in, so I hadn't been totally focused on the words of the ceremony. My attention had snapped back when I'd heard Fern compare marriage to a sale at Neiman's, but then he was pronouncing Leatrice and Sidney Allen man and wife, and we were all walking back down the aisle.

I spotted Fern and hurried over to him. "What was that?"

He took a small step back. "What do you mean?"

"I mean the wham-bam-thank-you-ma'am ceremony. Did you even ask them what you were supposed to ask to make it legal?"

He swatted a hand at me. "Of course it's legal. I am an ordained minister, Annabelle."

"By the internet," I said. "Hermès could get ordained online."

Fern giggled. "Now there's an idea. The Reverend Hermès Gerard. Ooo—he sounds like a proper Anglican priest. Wouldn't it be fun if I did joint ceremonies with the dog? I'll bet there are people who'd pay good money for that."

No people I wanted to meet, I thought as I spun around looking for Reese. We'd walked back down the aisle together, but he'd peeled off before we got to the house. I suspected he was having that conversation with Jimmy about why his own nephew was trying to kill him.

"I can't believe it," Richard said as he walked up and stared at his watch. "We're back on schedule."

"Not a huge shock since I allotted thirty minutes for the ceremony, and we blew through it in six."

Richard craned his neck and frowned. "I'll bet my waiters are still filling champagne glasses." He sighed and handed Hermès to me. "I'll have to get drinks for the bride and groom myself."

Hermès and I watched him flounce out the door and head for

the bar tucked under the large shade tree. Most of the guests were wisely standing under the leafy boughs of the tree, either waiting in line for a drink or just avoiding the sun.

Reese and his brother stood with Jimmy off to the side near the claw-foot bathtub filled with ice and bottled drinks. As they were talking, Detective Hobbes joined them. I noticed that he'd changed out of the frumpy suit he'd been wearing earlier and now wore an equally shapeless, but less wrinkled, dark suit.

"Ready for photos?" Kate asked. She looked unfazed by the heat and sun, her hair still smooth and held in place by a pair of butterflies, and her makeup flawless.

I dabbed at the sweat on my upper lip and shifted Hermès to my other arm. "Are we still doing them outside?"

"Outside is prettier than inside," she said. "Not to mention there's better light out there."

I knew she was right, but I hated leaving the comfort of the climate-controlled house. It also felt very strange to be on the other side of things. Usually at this point in a wedding, Kate and I were gathering items from the ceremony, putting final touches on the ballroom, and ensuring the bridal party had drinks for photos. It was also the time we took a quick breather after the hustle and bustle of getting the bride up and down the aisle. We chugged a soda, wolfed down an energy bar, and kicked off our shoes, if even for half an hour.

"No rest for the bridesmaids," Kate said, reading my mind as we herded the bridal party outside.

"Remind me not to be a bridesmaid again," I said, making sure I was out of earshot of Leatrice.

"What about being a bride?"

I suppressed a groan. "If this day is any indication of what I have to look forward to, I'm giving serious consideration to eloping."

"That's fine," Kate said as we walked up the brick path. "As long as you take all of us with you."

I didn't point out that taking a dozen people with me would

defeat the purpose of eloping. As I looked around at our motley crew lining up in front of the stone alcove for photos, I couldn't imagine getting married without any of them. I glanced down at Hermès, his tiny pink tongue hanging out of his mouth. Even the dog. I also couldn't imagine going through a wedding day as a bride.

"First we'll take a photo with the entire wedding party, and then we'll remove people for various groupings," the photographer said, swinging her sable-brown ponytail from side to side as she addressed everyone. She arranged Buster and Mack on either side of the newlyweds, taking great efforts to have them stand at an angle so she could fit everyone into the frame. "Can I have the flower girl and her attendant as well as the ring bearer duo?"

I hoped Richard never heard himself referred to as one half of a ring bearer duo, I thought as I waved both him and my fiancé over.

Richard carried a round silver tray of waters and champagne with him, which he set on a nearby armchair. "I hope we can make this fast. I still need to talk to the kitchen."

"I hope those are for us," Kate said, eyeing the drinks. "I am in serious need of a cocktail."

For once, I couldn't agree more. I handed Hermès off to Richard as the photographer directed him to stand next to me and moved Kate to the other side next to Fern.

"How did it go with Jimmy?" I asked Reese when he slid in place on the other side of me.

He put an arm around my waist. "Strange. Jimmy insists the man couldn't have been his nephew. Says his nephew isn't old enough to hold a gun."

"So the ID was wrong?" I asked, facing forward for the camera.

Reese shrugged then smiled as the photographer told us to hold the pose. "Or Jimmy was lying."

"Why would he lie?" I shifted my weight and angled one leg

in front of the other, tilting my chin out and down to be sure I didn't have a double chin in the photos.

"Another big smile," the photographer called out as she stood on a chair and clicked away.

"Who knows? We don't really know anything about this guy except what Leatrice told us, and she hasn't laid eyes on him in over sixty years. For all we know, Jimmy could still be in tight with the Mob, and this is all a ploy to get to Leatrice."

"After all this time?" I asked. "The Mob boss she jilted is supposed to be dead."

"Now lean in closer to each other," the photographer said as we all shimmied closer.

"So he says." Reese's mouth was so close to my ear that his words sent shivers down my spine. "Hobbes is running a check on that and on Jimmy before we get any deeper into this."

My pulse quickened from my fiancé being pressed up so close to me. I couldn't manage to get out any intelligible words.

"Have I mentioned how pretty you look?" Reese asked, his voice a deep purr. "I don't even mind Fern's crazy butterflies."

I cleared my throat and hoped my knees wouldn't buckle. We'd been living together for months, but his touch still made my legs turn to jelly. "Thanks. I like the way you look in a tux."

"Yeah?" he said, with a chuckle. "Should I keep it to wear around the apartment?"

"Oh, for heaven's sake," Richard said with a tortured sigh. "You do know I'm standing right beside you, don't you?"

My cheeks warmed, and I darted a glance to Richard on my other side. "Sorry."

"And if you really want to know, you should be wearing a three-button jacket, not a one," Richard said with a sniff. "I'd hate for you to repeat this style at your own wedding."

"Good to know." Reese looked down at his chest. "But I assumed you'd be helping me pick out the formal wear for my wedding."

Richard's head snapped over to Reese. "Me?"

"Annabelle and I haven't officially asked our wedding party, but I hoped you'd be a groomsman. It would mean a lot to both of us."

Richard's mouth fell open, and he made a strangled noise.

"We're looking forward and smiling," the photographer called.

Richard turned to the camera, clearing his throat as he did so.

"Is that a yes?" I asked through a plastered-on smile.

"That's great, everyone," the photographer said, lowering her camera. "Now if I can have just the bride and groom with the bridesmaids and groomsmen."

"Well, of course," Richard said, stepping away and blinking rapidly. "I had no...I mean, it would be my hon...Yes, you can count on me." He cleared his throat again. "Now, I'd better go check on the kitchen."

Before he could make his escape, Leatrice sucked in her breath so loudly I thought she might swallow her teeth. I followed her gaze as she gaped at a man standing near the side of the house. "Who is that?"

CHAPTER 13

"That's PJ," Richard said. When no one reacted, he added, "My significant other."

"I thought he was imaginary," Leatrice said, her eyes still riveted to the tall man with sandy-brown hair who looked to be in his thirties.

I turned to face Richard. "I thought he was your age."

"He *is* my age," Richard said, looking affronted.

Kate arched an eyebrow at him as she took a couple of goblets of water from the tray Richard had brought and passed them to the bride and groom. "Talk about wishful drinking."

"Count me in for that," Fern said, giggling at my assistant's mangled expression and helping her pass out waters.

"He's in my age range," Richard said.

"How wide is that range?" I asked, gratefully taking the glass of ice water Fern handed me. "Eighteen to fifty?"

Richard's cheeks flushed. "I'll have you know that age is only a number."

Fern hooked an arm through Richard's as he sized up PJ from afar. "Honey, you haven't seen *that* number in a long time."

Hermès leapt down from Richard's arms and scampered across the lawn to PJ, yipping happily when he reached the man and was scooped up from the ground. PJ raised a hand in a wave when he looked over and saw all of us staring at him.

"Oh, for heaven's sake," Richard said. "Don't terrify the man."

"Richard's right," I said. "Act normal, everyone." I glanced back at the group and caught sight of Fern in his cassock, Buster and Mack in their dress leather, and the bird's nest bobbing on Leatrice's head. This would be easier said than done.

"I'd better go check on him," Richard said. "He doesn't know a soul."

"And we need to go spritz the flowers downstairs," Mack said, leading Buster away along with Prue and Merry, who looked like she was ready for a nap or a meal. I didn't blame her.

"Can I get that bridesmaids and groomsmen photo?" the photographer asked, swiping a sweaty strand of hair off her forehead.

"Sorry." I took a quick sip of water and stepped back into place. "You'd think we'd be an easier bridal party since we're all in the industry. Well, most of us."

"It's okay," she said with a weary smile. "I'm used to it."

She didn't look old enough to sound as world worn as she did, but I knew working weddings added years pretty quickly. After moving us around a bit and reminding us to lower our bouquets, she snapped her photos and thanked us.

"Now the priest with the couple."

I didn't correct her as Fern preened, standing between the bride and groom with his hands in prayer position.

"I feel like this is sacrilegious," Kate whispered.

I blinked as his large gold cross glinted in the sunlight. "As long as he doesn't start taking confessions."

"Now a few with just the bride and groom."

"Being on the other side of things feels weird," I told Reese when the photographer stepped away with Leatrice and Sidney Allen to shoot photos of them under the tree. "I'm not sure I like it."

He put an arm around my waist. "I'm sure it will be better when you're the bride and not a bridesmaid."

I wasn't so sure, and the thought of being the focus of everyone's attention made my mouth go dry. I took a gulp of water. One of the things I loved about being a wedding planner was that I was always behind the scenes. In a world where people documented their every move online, I found the anonymity comforting.

"For sure," Kate said. "Being a bridesmaid is the worst. You have to wear a crazy getup someone else picks out; you can't get as drunk as you need to; and every single male guest thinks you're fair game."

I agreed with her on the outfit part. I'd be glad to toss this pillbox hat in the back of my closet for good.

"I don't know if I'd call this outfit crazy," Fern said, touching a finger to Kate's blue lapel. "I've seen much worse bridesmaids' dresses than these."

"They're so prim," Kate said, glancing down at the pencil skirt that covered her knees. "How am I supposed to flirt in this? By the way, where's Daniel? He promised to bring me a martini after the ceremony."

Reese twisted his body as he scanned the entire walled garden behind the house. "He was watching Jimmy."

"Were they with Hobbes?" I asked, watching guests mingle with the costumed performers as the jazz ensemble played in the background.

"Yes, do you see him?"

"No," I said, "but maybe they went inside. It is pretty hot out here."

"Since your best friend is catering, what are the chances we can get him to sneak us some hors d'oeuvres and drinks from the kitchen?" Reese asked.

I gave him a scandalized look. "Do my ears deceive me, or is a law enforcement officer trying to circumvent the rules?"

"If it means getting out of this heat in an all-black tux, then that would be a yes."

Before I could playfully scold him some more, I heard Leatrice screech. Whipping my head around, I saw her next to the large shade tree bending over a figure lying on the ground. It took me only a second to realize that the figure was Sidney Allen. The photographer ran toward us, her eyes wild.

"Someone call 9-1-1!"

Reese was already running across the lawn when Kate, Fern, and I gave chase. I patted my hips uselessly, since my phone wasn't on me. Another reason to hate bridesmaids dresses. No pockets.

"What happened?" I asked as I reached Leatrice and knelt down next to her. My fiancé was already loosening Sidney Allen's tie as he held his cell phone to his ear with his shoulder, giving the address to the emergency dispatcher.

"I don't know," Leatrice said, wringing her hands. "We were taking photos and he started to sway, then he collapsed."

I looked at Sidney Allen's flushed face. "It's the heat."

"And the corset," Kate added.

"Kate's right," I told Reese. "We need to get him out of the heat and out of that contraption he's wearing."

Reese nodded and glanced up at Leatrice. "Did he hit his head when he fell?"

"No, he kind of slumped down slowly, so I was able to hold him up and keep him from hitting the ground too hard." She choked back a sob. "Is he alive?"

"Definitely," Reese said, "but his pulse is elevated, so I think Annabelle's right. The best thing to do is cool him off."

Fern threw a glass of ice water at Sidney Allen's face, and we all jumped back as droplets splattered on us.

"What are you doing?" Kate asked.

"No, that's actually good," Reese said. "We need to cool him off fast."

"Then I'm your man," Fern said, heading for the tray of

waters we'd left behind. "No one tosses drinks in faces like I do."

Daniel Reese appeared next to his brother. "What's going on?"

"Possible heatstroke," my fiancé said. "We're going to move him inside and cool him down."

Daniel nodded and took a position across from Reese, both men putting their arms under Sidney Allen. A pair of costumed performers stepped out of the crowd, dropping their fake Tommy guns and sliding their hands under his legs. The men heaved him up and began moving in unison across the lawn toward the house with Fern running behind with a tray of ice water.

"Come on," I told Leatrice, helping her stand. "Once he cools down, the reception will get back on track, so no more crying and ruining your mascara."

"That's right," Kate put an arm around her. "You don't want Fern to fuss at you for spoiling all his hard work."

Leatrice put a hand to her damp face. "You really think my Sweetie Pie will be all right?"

"Absolutely," I said. "This isn't the first person we've had faint at a wedding."

"At least he didn't land on marble," Kate said, looking over Leatrice's bird's nest at me. "Remember the bridesmaid who passed out in the National Cathedral?"

"I remember the other bridesmaids stepping over her," I said.

"Good heavens," Leatrice said with a weak giggle. "Was she okay?"

"Perfectly fine," I said. "Although that couple didn't last very long. Wasn't it only a year before they split up?"

"Something like that," Kate said. "Way too soon for all the trouble of having a cathedral wedding."

I noticed that color had returned to Leatrice's cheeks since we'd distracted her with our wedding war stories. We walked into the back of the house and followed the voices to one of the rooms set up with period furnishings. Sidney Allen lay on the carpet next to a Federal-style dining table that displayed eighteenth century china and fake food. His shirt was open, and Reese was unhooking his black girdle. Fern had dipped a cocktail napkin into the cold water and was patting it on Sidney Allen's forehead.

As Reese released the last hook of the girdle, Sidney Allen's belly sprung free, and he let out a groan of relief. His eyes fluttered open, and he gazed up at everyone.

"How do you feel, Honey Bun?" Leatrice asked, sinking down next to him and taking his hand in hers.

"Dizzy," he said. "But I can finally breathe again."

"You collapsed outside," Reese said. "Do you remember?"

The entertainment diva raised a hand to his head. "I remember feeling warm and having a hard time catching my breath. And then I saw *him*."

"Who?" Leatrice asked.

Sidney Allen found Kate in the group, his eyes locking on hers. "The man who forced his way into Leatrice's apartment. The one Kate fended off with her stun gun."

CHAPTER 14

The black girdle had been tossed over to the side, and the groom sat up drinking one of the glasses of ice water Fern had not been able to throw in his face, due to the fact that it would soak the antique rug and not because of any restraint on Fern's part.

"You saw the guy I stunned?" Kate asked, looking around the room as if he might be hiding behind one of the antique chairs. "Here? At the wedding?"

Fern made the sign of the cross with his one free hand and whispered to me, "The heat must be making the poor dear see things."

I was inclined to agree with Fern. I hadn't seen a dangerous looking Mob thug, although all our costumed performers weren't making it easy to spot a real threat.

"Where?" Reese asked Sidney Allen. Either he believed the groom or was doing an excellent job of humoring him.

"Standing on the side patio near the corner of the house. At first I thought I might be seeing things because I was feeling a little dizzy, but then he saw me across the lawn, and I knew it was the man who'd burst into my Sugar Muffin's apartment looking for Jimmy."

"Where is Jimmy?" I asked, looking around the assembled faces.

"I left him with Hobbes downstairs," Daniel Reese said.

His brother stood and exchanged a serious look with him. "We should make sure he's secure."

"What should we do?" Kate asked. "My stun gun is downstairs with my purse."

"Nothing," Reese said a bit too forcefully. "I don't want an armed bridal party roaming the place."

"Don't be so sure." Kate waggled a finger at him. "We had a wedding in Georgetown where the groom and all his groomsmen were with the Secret Service, and it proved to be very helpful when cars parked illegally in front of the church. You've never seen tow trucks arrive so quickly in your life."

Daniel grinned. "That I would have liked to see."

Reese turned to me. "Can you make sure your team doesn't stun anyone else while Daniel and I go check things out?"

"I'll try," I said. "Luckily, we need to get cocktails wrapped up and guests moved down to the ballroom for dinner. That should keep us busy. Wedding guests never move quickly."

Reese gave me a quick peck on the cheek, and he and Daniel ducked out of the room.

"What is everyone doing in here?" Richard's shrill voice carried from the foyer as the door to the back garden opened and closed.

I stepped out of the room to intercept him, but he peered in nonetheless.

"Getting Sidney Allen out of his girdle," Fern said in a stage whisper, motioning to the pile of shiny black fabric.

Richard looked at the discarded waist shaper, then at the dozen people gathered around Sidney Allen, including a pair of performers who looked like they should be carrying violin cases. "It took all of you to get it off?" He closed his eyes and put up his palms. "Never mind. I don't want to know."

"We were on our way outside," I said. "Are cocktails still going strong?"

"If by going strong you mean are people drinking water like they're running a marathon, then yes. Thank goodness I insisted on the lavender lemonade station. It's too hot for champagne."

"Bite your tongue," Fern said, looking as if he'd been slapped.

Richard ignored him. "I don't know if we should keep guests outside for a full hour. I don't want them to start dropping like flies."

"Too late," Kate mumbled.

The front door at the other end of the foyer swung open, and a pair of paramedics stepped inside.

"Down here." I waved at them, pointing inside the room where Leatrice sat next to her fiancé, fanning him with her bouquet as he sipped his water. "He's better now, but can you check his vitals?"

"Taking off his girdle my foot." Richard gave Fern a withering glance. "I suppose it wouldn't be a Wedding Belles wedding without at least one emergency vehicle."

I shushed him. "Don't say that so loud. I don't want people thinking that about our weddings."

"I think the rat's out of the bag on that one, Annabelle," Kate said, joining me in the foyer with Richard. "People know about all the murders we've been connected to."

"It's 'the cat's out of the bag'," Richard said.

Kate snorted. "Why would you put a cat in a bag? That makes no sense. A rat, however. . ."

Richard pivoted away from my assistant. "The point is, you have been around more than the usual number of murders at weddings."

"What is the usual number?" Fern asked, drumming his fingers on his chin as he joined us.

"I think that would be none," Kate said.

"Not all of the murders took place at the actual weddings," I insisted. "Some were before or after. I can count the ones that had dead bodies *at* the weddings on one hand."

Kate raised an eyebrow. "There's something to put in our ads."

"Look at the bright side, darling," Richard said. "At least the coroner's van isn't rolling up. Yet."

I pointed a finger at him. "And it won't. No one is dying today."

My friends didn't look convinced.

"I'm serious," I said. "This is our friend's wedding, and we're going to make sure no one gets knocked off on our watch."

"We, as in the four of us?" Fern asked, scanning our small group and nibbling the corner of his mouth.

"We also have Reese and his brother," I said. "And Buster and Mack."

Kate tilted her head at me, and her decorative butterfly flopped to one side. "Didn't your hot hubby-to-be just tell us not to do anything?"

"He said not to stun anyone," I said. "He didn't say anything about not looking for the guys who are after Jimmy. If the hit man who was looking for him earlier is actually here, we need to find him before he finds Jimmy. And Reese said another man flew into DC with Jimmy's nephew. He might be here too."

"Two hit men?" Richard asked, his face paling under his bronzer.

"Maybe," I said, "but Sidney Allen claims he only saw one. The other one could be the wheel man."

Fern glanced toward the front door. "But won't this Mob guy be armed? What do we do if he shoots at us?"

"He's not going to shoot at us," I said.

"That's right," Kate said. "If he's in the Mob, he's more likely to strangle us or throw us into a river so we can sleep with the fishes."

Fern's fingers flew to his neck. "I think I'd rather be shot."

I glared at my assistant. "No one is going to get shot or strangled. If we see anyone who looks like the Mob hit man, we find Reese."

"Half the guests here look like Mob hit men," Richard said as the two costumed performers who'd helped carry Sidney Allen inside passed us and went back outside.

I had to admit that our plan to help Jimmy the Pencil blend in with the crowd may have backfired on us. "I guess if they look too stereotypical, they're probably in costume. I don't think members of the modern Mafia walk around in spats."

"More's the pity," Fern said.

"Mob hit man or no Mob hit man," Richard said, "I still have dinner service to worry about. Plus, I have to make sure PJ doesn't get wind of this. I haven't filled him in on how my best friend is a murder magnet."

"He doesn't know about any of it?" Kate's mouth gaped. "Not even when you were a murder suspect?"

Richard shrugged. "He travels a lot."

It wasn't my place to judge relationships. I'd learned long ago that I was better at planning weddings than predicting the success of them. You never knew what magic ingredient made some couples stick together and why others flamed out, so who was I to say that Richard's relationship was unusual? I'd met my fiancé when I'd tripped over a dead mother of the bride, so I tried not to throw stones from my glass house.

"Why don't I go downstairs with Richard so he can touch base with the kitchen, and I can get Buster and Mack to help us?" I said, looking at the paramedics packing up to leave and Sidney Allen standing next to Leatrice. "Fern, can you keep the happy couple entertained until dinner? I don't want Leatrice worrying or Sidney Allen passing out again."

Fern gave me a sharp salute that seemed out of step with his priest's cassock. "On it."

"What do you want me to do?" Kate asked.

"You're with me," I said, waving for her to follow me down the stairs.

We descended to the lower level, passing through the offices and reaching the ballroom. Buster and Mack spritzed the center-pieces with water from plastic spray bottles while waiters filled water goblets. I expected to see my fiancé and his brother, as well as Hobbes and Jimmy the Pencil, but they weren't there.

"Careful, people," Richard said, clapping his hands loudly and making a few waiters jump. "These are not quick-dry linens, so no spilling."

"Hey, guys," I called to Buster and Mack. "Did you see where Reese and his brother went?"

"They would have been with Detective Hobbes and the gray-haired man in the double-breasted suit and fedora," Kate added.

Mack paused his spraying. "Reese and Daniel were here, but they left right away."

"Something about Jimmy being missing and Hobbes not answering his phone," Buster said. "I assumed you knew."

"That's it," Kate said, weaving her way through the clear reception chairs. "I'm getting my stun gun."

CHAPTER 15

"**I** am not going to be happy with you if you stun me," I said, looking over my shoulder as Kate followed me with her stun gun in one hand.

She gave the flashlight-cum-stun-gun a wave. "You'll be happy when I fend off an armed attacker."

I paused with my fingers on the handle of one of the French doors that led out to the lower patio. "We're going to be circulating through what's left of cocktail hour, so gun down."

Kate grumbled but lowered her weapon. Apparently, my fiancé and his brother had left through these doors, so I figured following them was the quickest way to find them. We'd sent Buster and Mack outside to see if there was, indeed, a second hit man waiting in a getaway car. If anyone could intimidate a mobster, it would be them.

We left the ballroom and crossed the patio to a set of stone steps. A waiter descended with a silver tray of picked-over hors d'oeuvres, and Kate snagged him by the arm, plucking off a miniature quiche.

"Goat cheese," she said, closing her eyes and sighing as she chewed. "You've got to try them."

"We're on a mission," I said. "We don't have time to eat."

Kate threw her hands up. "We never get to eat. When we're the wedding planners, we're always too busy to eat until the food's cold. Now that we're actually bridesmaids, you still aren't going to let me eat? Do you plan to starve me at your wedding too?"

I stopped and looked at her, then looked at the waiter shifting uncomfortably. I took a baby quiche and popped it into my mouth. Even though it was no longer hot, the crust was buttery and the goat cheese had a refreshing tang. Richard really did do pastry well.

"Happy?" I asked after I swallowed.

"Getting there." Kate took the last quiche and the waiter moved away, no doubt grateful to get away from our spat. "So what's the deal with your wedding? You've been engaged for months and haven't started planning yet. I think you could get kicked out of the wedding planner's alliance for something like that."

"There's no such thing as a wedding planner's alliance," I said as we started up the stairs. "And you know how busy we've been with summer weddings."

Kate hiked her skirt up so she could take the steps two at a time. "But the season's over, and it's July. You should at least pick a date."

When we reached the top of the steps, I surveyed the garden. Guests still mingled under the tree and near the bar, and more than one person stood dipping their hands into the clawfoot tub filled with rapidly melting ice. The swing ensemble played, the lead singer crooning into an old-fashioned microphone, but Jimmy the Pencil wasn't with them.

Luckily, the sun had dipped below the tree line, so the heat was no longer so oppressive. I spotted Leatrice and Sidney Allen holding court on one of the vintage sofas on the lawn, and was pleased both looked like they were enjoying themselves. I wondered where Fern was since I didn't notice his black cassock flapping in the breeze anywhere.

"Next summer," I said after I failed to locate Reese or his brother.

"That's vague," Kate said.

"Well, not June, that's for sure. We're already booked for most of June. It will have to be one of the off-season months like July or August."

"You know there's a reason they're off-season, right?" Kate asked as we made our way across the lawn toward the back door. "Might I remind you of the lovely weather in DC in July and August?"

"Who said I'm getting married in DC?"

Kate stumbled and caught herself on my arm. "Seriously? Are we talking a destination wedding, because I've got tons of ideas of amazing places for an island wedding? Or a Tuscan villa. Or maybe the coast of Spain. "

"Who knows?" I shrugged. "I'm keeping my options open and letting the wind take me where it will."

Kate eyed me. "That doesn't sound like you at all. This is just your way of jerking me around, isn't it? You haven't given it any thought at all."

I paused when we reached the door. "Right now I'm focused on making sure this wedding does not have a body count. Then I'll think about my own wedding."

Another waiter passed, and Kate lifted two glasses of champagne off his tray without him noticing. She pressed one in my hand. "That's the problem. There's always a reason why you can't focus on yourself. If it isn't Leatrice's wedding, it will be someone else's. Pretty soon we'll start finalizing fall weddings, then it will be fall season, and then it's the mad rush to the holidays. I know you're used to keeping your nose to the grime stone, but when will it ever be your turn?"

"Grindstone," I corrected her, cringing a little at the thought of a *grime* stone and having my nose figuratively pressed to it.

She let out an impatient sigh. "You know what I mean, Annabelle. You always know what I mean. And don't try to change the subject. Why are you so scared to be the one getting married? Is it your absurd notion that you can't be the one in the spotlight because you're supposed to be the person taking care of everyone else?"

I took a gulp of champagne to wash away the lump that had formed in my throat. I hated how right she was and how well she knew me.

Kate tapped one toe on the patio. "Do you want to marry him?"

"What?" I nearly choked on my champagne. "You know I do."

"Then you'd better start acting like it. I know Reese adores you and is used to you being a crazy career girl, but you can't always put him and your relationship second. Marriage doesn't work that way."

"When did you become an expert in marriage?" I asked, knowing she had never come even remotely close to being engaged or even very serious about the many men she dated.

She looked at me like I was an idiot. "We do work with people who're getting married every single day. Plus, I watch a lot of the Oprah channel."

"Do you think Reese is upset I haven't started planning yet?" I asked, keeping my voice low as a pair of flappers walked by waving their long cigarette holders at us.

Kate tossed back the rest of her bubbly. "Lucky for you, he's laid-back, but I think he probably expected his wedding planner fianceé to have done a little more planning at this point."

The thought that I might have hurt his feelings made tears sting the backs of my eyes. "You're right. I'm being ridiculous and impractical. I know better than anyone that it takes a year to plan a DC wedding, even during an off month. And I do want to marry him sooner rather than later."

"Of course you do. He's a hunky cop who thinks your lack of cooking skill and aversion to housekeeping is cute. If it were me, I'd have eloped already before he came to his senses."

I laughed. "Starting Monday, you're in charge of my wedding planning."

"Me?" Kate put a hand to her chest.

"Well, I'm not asking Fern or Richard. They'd give me anxiety attacks, and Fern would make me wear a dress covered in swan feathers. But I do need someone to light a fire under me."

Kate threw an arm around my shoulder. "Consider me your personal fire starter. Of course, Fern might still try to cover you in swan feathers."

I finished my champagne and handed the empty glass to a waiter I saw approaching from the corner of my eye.

Kate's eyes grew wide. "Um, Annabelle. That's not a waiter."

I twisted slightly and found myself face-to-face with Richard's significant other. "Oh my gosh." I reached for the glass as my cheeks burned with embarrassment. "I'm so sorry. I saw your white dinner jacket and thought you were one of Richard's waiters, even though they're wearing white shirts and bistro aprons. Obviously, you don't look like them. Your jacket's much nicer. Not that the waiters don't look nice. Please don't tell Richard I said his waiters didn't look nice."

The man grinned at me. "You're Annabelle."

I nodded mutely, very aware that if I opened my mouth again, I might start babbling senselessly.

An actual waiter passed by, and PJ put my empty glass on his tray.

"I'm Kate." Kate held out her hand as she shamelessly sized him up. "It's nice to finally meet you."

"You too." PJ shook both of our hands. "Richard has told me all about both of you."

"Really?" I wondered if that included his many opinions about my lack of style and Kate's lack of modesty.

"He's been pretty secretive about you." Kate put a hand on his arm and leaned in. "Do you really work for the State Department?"

PJ nodded, running a hand through his sandy hair. "Guilty as charged."

"What's that like? Richard says you jet all over the world." Kate gave him the smile she usually used to charm men into submission.

"Not as exciting as it sounds. Long flights. Even longer meetings."

"I'll bet," Kate said.

I spotted Richard across the lawn and saw the moment that he located us. Even from fifty feet away, I could see him assess the situation and press his lips together in disapproval.

I pulled Kate away from PJ, giving him an apologetic smile. "We have to run check on things for dinner, but I hope we'll see you later."

Before he could respond or Kate could protest, I jerked her inside the house and closed the door behind us.

"That was a bit rude," Kate said, wrenching her arm from my grasp.

"I was saving you," I said. "Richard saw you in full-flirt mode."

Kate's cheeks flushed. "Oops. You know I have a hard time turning it off. I see a cute guy, and it's automatic."

"Oh, I'm aware." It didn't bother me when Kate smiled a little too brightly at my fiancé, but I knew Richard wasn't so forgiving. "We also need to keep looking for Jimmy."

The door to one of the nearby exhibit rooms opened and Fern emerged, his priest garb replaced by a white double-breasted suit with a black pinstripe. His black fedora was pulled down at an angle. So much for resuming our search posthaste.

"What happened to Father Fern?" Kate asked.

"He was wilting," Fern said. "All black in this heat? Girl, please." He glanced at my hair. "Where are you two off to? I don't suppose you'd let me refresh your hair?"

"Refresh my hair?" I asked. "I'm afraid to ask what that entails."

He fluttered a hand at my head. "Take out the hat, add more butterflies, maybe a baby bluebird."

"Hard pass," I said. "We're actually looking for Reese and his brother, who were looking for Detective Hobbes and Jimmy."

"I don't know about your hottie cop, but I did see Jimmy heading upstairs with someone."

I exchanged a quick look with Kate. "Was the someone Hobbes?"

Fern pursed his lips. "Which one is Hobbes?"

"A little pudgy with light hair," I said. "He's dating Alexandra."

His face remained blank.

"He's got the comb-over you're always dying to fix," Kate added.

"Yes!" Fern snapped his fingers. "I know who you mean now."

"So was it him with Jimmy?" I asked.

He shook his head. "Nope. This guy was younger with better hair."

I knew Fern hadn't seen the Mob hit man who'd been in Leatrice's apartment, so I didn't bother asking. "They went upstairs? Was Jimmy being dragged?"

Fern shook his head. "He and the other guy looked as thick as thieves." He waved for us to follow him back inside. "Come on. I'll show you where I saw them last."

Kate looked at me. "If Jimmy went willingly, do you think that means he's been scamming us this entire time?"

"You mean being a Trojan horse to get close to Leatrice?" My heart beat faster. "If that's the case, get ready to light him up too."

Kate held her stun gun higher. "Gladly."

"Should we bring backup?" I asked, wishing for a hundredth time that day that my dress had a pocket for my phone so I could call Reese. "If Jimmy's a bad guy, it will be two of them against three of us, and only one of us is armed."

Kate waved her stun gun. "This is our backup. Besides, we have no idea where your fiancé and Daniel ran off to."

I knew she was right, but also held out hope that the two men were currently searching the second floor. We started up the stairs. The period oil paintings on the walls of the staircase landing gave way to bright-white walls at the top, and I remembered that the interactive historical exhibits were on the second floor.

Fern paused before proceeding up the rest of the stairs. "The last place I saw them was on this landing heading up."

"Why would they have come up here?" I whispered as we walked the rest of the way. The space felt deserted since guests were not usually allowed on this floor during weddings.

"Maybe because no one is up here?" Kate whispered back.

All four doors off the landing were closed, and I crooked a finger for Kate and Fern to follow me as I peeked into the one closest to us. The room was light and airy with one curved wall that overlooked the front lawn. Framed art hung on the wall, and a pair of white screens stood in the center of the room covered with more images.

I shook my head and pulled the door closed as quietly as I could. Fern was already opening the door across the hall, so Kate and I shuffled behind him. This room was actually a narrow hallway with a black-and-white checkered floor that led into another small room.

Fern peeked his head through the doorframe and sucked in air.

"I was hoping you'd join us," the man said.

Over Fern's shoulder, I saw Jimmy the Pencil standing next to a broad-shouldered man. Kate stiffened next to me. Although he looked different standing up as opposed to lying sprawled on the floor, there was no doubt who it was.

Not only had we found Jimmy, we'd found the hit man who was looking for him.

CHAPTER 16

"Don't think I won't stun you again," Kate said, holding her weapon out.

The man pulled a gun from a holster under his jacket. "I'm sure you'll try."

Fern squeaked and tried to back out, treading on my toes in the process. I winced and wished I'd changed out of the strappy, high-heeled sandals I'd worn for the ceremony.

"Where did you get that?" Kate asked, staring at the gun. "You didn't have it earlier."

"My associate usually carries the weapons. Now, please." The man waved us in with his gun. "I insist. We have lots to discuss."

I reluctantly entered the small room, made even smaller by the wall of gray fabric that covered the window. To one side of the two men was a tall Plexiglas display that held blueprints that were clearly part of the exhibit. Aside from that, and two panels of wall text, the room was bare and smelled slightly of old books. I didn't see any associate, which made me wonder if even more mobsters were wandering around the wedding.

"Are you okay, Jimmy?" I asked the older man.

"I think so," he said. "I don't know why I'm up here though."

"'Course he's okay," the other man clapped a heavy hand on his shoulder. "I wouldn't hurt my own uncle."

"So you are his nephew," I said, although knowing the two men were technically related didn't make me feel much better.

The man gave a curt nod. "I'm Vinnie."

Fern put his hands over his ears. "I didn't hear anything. I don't know your name."

Vinnie gave Fern a curious look. "It seems you folks have got the wrong idea about me."

"Oh really?" Kate asked, her flashlight stun gun still clutched in her hand. "Are you going to tell me you didn't burst into our friend's apartment looking for Jimmy?"

He shrugged. "No, but I wasn't looking for him to whack him."

Fern jumped at the word 'whack' but didn't drop his hands from his ears.

"So we're supposed to believe it was a social call?" Kate said. "You weren't exactly friendly."

"I'd just flown halfway across the country in economy class in the middle seat. What kind of mood would you be in?"

"Well, that explains it." Fern lowered his hands. "I'd be homicidal myself."

I shot Fern a look.

Vinnie pointed his gun at Kate. "This one didn't give me a chance to explain before she lit me up."

"That's right," Kate said pointing her stun gun right back at him. "And I'll do it again."

I let out a breath. "Can everyone lower the guns for a minute? It's impossible to listen with a gun being waved in your face."

"Fine." Vinnie waited until Kate had lowered her arm before he put his gun back into the holster. "Happy?"

"That wouldn't be the first word that would come to mind," Fern muttered.

"So if we got it all wrong, why don't you tell us why you flew across the country to chase after your uncle?" I said.

"Family looks out for family," Vinnie said, looking over at his uncle. "And Uncle Jimmy, well he's been getting confused for a while now. It wasn't so bad when my aunt could watch out for him, but when she passed it got worse. He wanders off and forgets where he lives. Lately, he's even been forgetting his own kids and is convinced someone is trying to kill him."

I glanced over at Jimmy, who looked more confused than ever. "Are you telling me the family isn't after him?"

Vinnie chuckled and shook his head. "Why would we be after him? Uncle Jimmy hasn't done the books for over a decade. Anyway, the new boss is going legit, so we got nothing to hide."

Jimmy scratched his head. "Frank's boy isn't after me?"

Vinnie put a hand on his uncle's arm. "No, Uncle Jimmy. Everyone just wants you back home safe."

I knew a good con man could pull the wool over anyone's eyes, but Vinnie seemed to genuinely care about the old man. Dementia would certainly explain why Jimmy kept wandering off, and why he spontaneously decided to sing with the band. Suddenly, the old man's confusion made sense.

"How do we know you aren't making this up so you can waltz out of here with him?" Kate asked.

Vinnie reached into his breast pocket and produced a sheaf of folded papers. "Take a look yourself. His latest doctor's report."

I took the papers and unfolded them, scanning the text quickly. They seemed to come from a doctor at the University of Chicago Medical Center, and they did declare that one James Constantine Pinnello was suffering from advanced cortical dementia. Kate read over my shoulder and gave a tiny gasp.

"He was pretty convincing. He convinced our friend too." I didn't mention that he'd also convinced her to illegally procure forged documents on the dark web for him.

"Sometimes his made-up stories seem more real than the truth," Vinnie said. "Trust me. I know."

"But how did he find our friend and make his way across the country if all this is accurate?" Kate asked, waving a hand at the paper.

"He remembers the past like it was yesterday," Vinnie said. "Never forgets a name if he knew them fifty years ago. He might not remember yours tomorrow, though."

"That would make sense," I said. "He knew our friend a long time ago."

"And he still remembers how to do things like buy a plane ticket and call a taxi," Vinnie explained. "Which is why we try to keep an eye on him, so he doesn't drive to a house someone lived in thirty years ago."

"Did you know Leelee has been in the same apartment building for over twenty years?" Jimmy asked.

Actually, I didn't, although I knew it had been a long time.

"That explains it," Fern said. "He kept track of her."

Jimmy nodded. "We were always good friends."

Vinnie patted his hand. "I hope my uncle didn't disrupt the wedding too much. We'll get out of your hair."

"I don't understand," Jimmy said, looking at us then at his nephew. "I thought I was going to a wedding."

A lump lodged in my throat, and I blinked hard a few times as I handed the papers back to Vinnie. "It looks like your family back in Chicago misses you."

"But I was going to have wedding cake," Jimmy said.

"I'll get you cake in the airport," Vinnie said.

Jimmy didn't look convinced and folded his arms across his chest. "It's rude to leave a wedding before the bride and groom cut the cake."

"He's got you there," Fern said.

"Why don't you both stay?" I said. "Richard already added one seat for dinner. I'm sure he can add another."

"I can't wait to see the look on his face when you tell him," Kate muttered under her breath.

Vinnie raised an eyebrow at me. "You've got a bunch of cops

looking for me. And I did leave police custody. I don't expect the DC police look real kindly on that type of thing."

Fern fluttered a hand at him. "Don't you worry about that. Our Annabelle has an in with them since she's engaged to their top detective."

I wasn't sure Reese would like to hear that Fern thought I had an "in" with the police department, but I knew I could explain things to him. "I think I can smooth that over."

Vinnie cracked a smile for the first time since we'd been talking. "It would make him easier to deal with. Lately, he gets real upset when he doesn't get his way."

Kate elbowed me and whispered, "If that's a symptom, have we considered that Richard may have dementia?"

"Let's get you both downstairs and seated while I talk to my fiancé," I said, motioning for Vinnie and Jimmy to follow me.

"You look familiar," Jimmy said as he fell in step with Fern. "Have we met?"

Fern patted his hand. "I performed the ceremony, sweetie."

Jimmy took in his white suit and fedora. "You're a Catholic priest?"

Fern giggled. "Not by a long shot. I'm a hairdresser."

Jimmy furrowed his brow. This was doing nothing for the old man's confusion.

"Do you think they'll let me sing again?" Jimmy finally asked Fern.

"I don't see why not," Fern said. "Leatrice isn't a real stickler for things being by the book."

I led the way downstairs, where we met Reese and his brother on their way up. My fiancé did a double take and one hand went instinctively to the gun that wasn't on his hip.

I held up both hands. "Whoa. It's not what you think, and I can explain everything."

Reese looked from Vinnie to Jimmy to me. "Why do I have a feeling this is going to be a doozy?"

The front door flew open, and Buster and Mack strode in

with a dark-haired man held snugly between them. "Look who we found waiting in a rented car down the block."

"They pulled me out of the car and tackled me," the man said, a stunned expression on his face I hoped wasn't a result of being tackled too hard.

"Only because you ran," Mack said.

The man looked between the two burly florists. "Who wouldn't?"

"Is this your associate?" Reese asked Vinnie.

"This is Carmine," Vinnie said. "Our new accountant. I brought him with me because Jimmy trained him, so they know each other real well. The more familiar faces, the better."

Mack and Buster relaxed their grip and exchanged a worried look over the man's disheveled hair.

"We apprehended an accountant?" Mack said.

"Why are the wedding florists pulling people out of cars?" Reese asked, his gaze boring into me. "I could have sworn I said that I didn't want the bridal party to get involved."

Kate slipped her stun gun behind her back. "Then you're not going to like this explanation very much."

CHAPTER 17

"I did not see this coming," Kate said, her eyes on the dance floor.

"You mean you didn't think our eighty-something-year-old bride would have a father-daughter dance?" I asked as Jimmy the Pencil spun Leatrice out and back in to the sounds of Frank Sinatra's "The Way You Look Tonight."

Fern leaned over from his seat further down the table. "Who knew accountants could dance so well?"

Reese draped his arm across the back of my chair. "The addition of a father-daughter dance is the least surprising part of this entire day."

"You can say that again," Richard said, poking his head over Reese. "I still can't believe you made me add four seats to the head table. We're packed in here like sardines."

I glanced down the long oval table tightly ringed with clear reception chairs, the tall palm fronds rising high enough off the table that I could see clearly underneath them. We'd planned for fourteen of us around Leatrice and Sidney Allen's table, but Leatrice had insisted on adding Jimmy, Carmine, and Vinnie, and then Kate had insisted with equal passion on adding Daniel next to her.

Richard had thrown a modified hissy fit—shortened only because of the heat and his relief that dinner service wouldn't be interrupted by gunfire—but had finally relented. So now my eyes went from Kate to Daniel, who looked cozier than seemed appropriate, to Fern, who'd removed his black fedora, to Buster and Mack with baby Merry in a booster seat with Prue on the other side. Detective Hobbes sat next to Alexandra, and he seemed as surprised as anyone to have the sexy cake baker nuzzled up to him. We'd put the three mobsters next to Hobbes, with the theory that he could keep an eye on them just in case. Looking at the detective's dazed expression made me realize we hadn't thought that through. Luckily, Alexandra and Hobbes were too distracted to notice that, on the other side of Jimmy the Pencil, Hermès sat in a booster seat between PJ and Richard. Leatrice's and Sidney Allen's chairs between Richard and Reese were empty since both were on the dance floor—Leatrice spinning around with Jimmy and Sidney Allen waiting anxiously to cut in. Aside from the few empty chairs, we were shoulder to shoulder, not that anyone seemed to mind.

"How was your first experience as a best man?" I asked, snuggling closer to Reese.

"A lot more dramatic than I expected, although I guess I should have known that one of your weddings wouldn't be a walk in the park."

"I'll have you know that, despite all the craziness, the reception has been perfectly on time." I elbowed him playfully. "But, seriously, thanks for being so understanding and for dropping the charges against Vinnie."

"We should be grateful he didn't press charges against Kate since she did stun him."

"I guess you're right. Should we call the wedding a success? No shots were fired, and no one was arrested."

Reese rapped the edge of the table with his knuckles. "Knock on wood. We still have an hour to go."

"As far as I'm concerned," Richard said, leaning over the empty seats between him and Reese, "it's all downhill from here. Entrée is cleared, and the only thing left on the schedule is the cake cutting, which has little to do with my kitchen."

"So no chef walkouts this time?" I asked.

"No, thank heavens. Chefs can be so melodramatic." Richard fanned himself with one hand. "You have no idea what it's like to work with that level of hysteria."

Reese raised an eyebrow at me, but neither of us responded. I reached for my champagne flute and took a sip, waving back to Leatrice with my other hand as she spun around the dance floor.

"It's time for everyone to join the bride and groom on the dance floor," the bandleader announced as they shifted into another classic ballad.

Reese held out his hand. "Shall we?"

Even though it felt strange to be walking onto the dance floor instead of standing off to the side holding a wedding day time-line, I took his hand and followed him.

We weren't the only ones joining Leatrice and Sidney Allen as the band sang "It Had To Be You." I spotted Kate pulling Daniel behind her, and Alexandra and Hobbes swaying so close there was no daylight between them. Buster danced with Prue while Mack was right beside them with baby Merry.

"Isn't this the best day ever?" Leatrice called to me as Sidney Allen twirled her past us.

I laughed. If the bride and groom were happy, I guessed I could count it as a success.

"So you never told me what it was like being a bridesmaid," Reese said as we moved across the floor.

"Odd," I admitted. "It feels strange to be a guest. I'm so used to being on the other side of things that even dancing with you like this feels bizarre."

"So has being a wedding planner ruined weddings for you forever?"

"I wouldn't say ruined, but my perspective is definitely different. To the rest of the world, a wedding means booze and dancing and getting dressed up. To me, it means forgetting to eat for ten hours, wearing flats with gel inserts so I'm not limping the next day, and fending off drunk groomsmen."

"Is that why you're not excited about planning our wedding?"

I looked up at him and nearly tripped over his feet. "Who told you I wasn't excited?"

"Babe." He smoothed a loose strand of hair off my forehead. "No one had to tell me. You haven't wanted to set a date, and you get a panicky look on your face every time I mention it."

"What panicky look—?" I started to say.

He pointed at me. "That one. Like you're looking for some-place to run and hide."

I clamped my mouth shut. He knew me too well. I did want to run off and hide or at least change the subject.

"If our wedding isn't going to be fun for you, we can elope," he said. "I don't need the traditional wedding if it's going to make you miserable."

I pressed my head against his chest, the warmth and solid-ness of him making me feel better. I also didn't want Reese to see that I was about to cry. Not because I was overwhelmed by the idea of being a bride, but because I was overwhelmed that he'd do anything to make me happy. Kate was right. I needed to marry this guy fast.

The music changed and the tempo picked up. I saw Fern dash across the dance floor and cut in on Leatrice and Sidney Allen.

"They're playing our song," he said as he took Leatrice by the hand.

"Is that 'Dancing Queen' by Abba?" I asked, recognizing the opening of the song.

"I'm surprised a jazz band knows it," Reese said.

I eyed Fern as he jubilantly danced with Leatrice, twirling and dipping her. "I suspect this might have been planned ahead of time."

"I thought Fern was the anti-planning planner."

"Not when it comes to having a showcase dance with the bride," I said. "I'm just glad he didn't change into a bell bottom jumpsuit for it."

"When in Rome," Reese said, spinning me away from him and back in.

I laughed as I braced one hand against his chest. "Since when can you dance disco?"

He winked at me as he did a passable imitation of John Travolta in *Saturday Night Fever*. "I'm full of surprises, babe."

I noticed Jimmy the Pencil dancing with one of the cigarette girls, and Vinnie cutting in on a flustered Hobbes. Richard and PJ spun past us holding Hermès between them, his tiny pink tongue hanging happily from his mouth. For the first time all day, I felt totally happy.

"You know what?" I said, looking up at my fiancé. "We should have a wedding. And not an elopement. A real wedding with a bridal party and dancing and all the craziness."

"Are you sure?"

I nodded. "Positive. Weddings are about being with the people you love when you say 'I Do' to the person you love most. And I can't imagine getting married without all of my crazy friends. Mobsters not included."

Reese grinned and looked around the dance floor. "It would be sad to miss all this." His face became serious. "You don't think Fern will want a spotlight dance with you, do you?"

"What do you think?" I asked. "You'll be lucky if he doesn't want one with you."

Reese shook his head. "Maybe you were right about eloping."

"You know you love them," I said.

Reese's mouth twitched up into a smile. "You're right. As crazy as they all are, they're a part of you, and I love every single bit of you."

"You say that now," I told him, standing on my tiptoes to give him a quick kiss. "But you haven't met my mother."

ALSO BY LAURA DURHAM

Read the entire Annabelle Archer Series in order:

Better Off Wed

For Better Or Hearse

Dead Ringer

Review To A Kill

Death On The Aisle

Night of the Living Wed

Eat, Prey, Love

Groomed For Murder

Wed or Alive

To Love and To Perish

Marry & Bright

The Truffle with Weddings

Irish Aisles are Smiling

Godfather of Bride

To get notices whenever I release a new book, follow me on BookBub:

https://www.bookbub.com/profile/laura-durham

Did you enjoy this book? You can make a big difference!

I'm extremely lucky to have a loyal bunch of readers, and honest reviews are the best way to help bring my books to the attention of new readers.

If you enjoyed *Godfather of the Bride*, I would be forever grateful if you could spend two minutes leaving a review (it can be as short as you like) on your favorite retailer.

Thanks for reading and reviewing!

ACKNOWLEDGMENTS

As always, an enormous thank you to all of my wonderful readers, especially my beta readers and my review team. I never give you enough time, but you always come through for me. A special shout-out to the beta readers who caught all my goofs this time: Patricia Joyner, Linda Reachill, Sheila Kraemer, Lisa Hudson, Linda Loy, Lind Fore, Karen Diamond, Tricia Knox, Toni, Katherine Munro, Sandra Anderson, Tony Noice, Elizabeth Brown, and Annemarie Pasquale. Thank you!!

A big thank you to my wonderful copyeditor Sandy Chance and my creative cover designer Keri Knutson.

Big kisses to everyone who leaves reviews. They really make a difference, and I am grateful for every one of them!

ABOUT THE AUTHOR

Laura Durham has been writing for as long as she can remember and has been plotting murders since she began planning weddings over twenty years ago in Washington, DC. Her first novel, BETTER OFF WED, won the Agatha Award for Best First Novel.

When she isn't writing or wrangling brides, Laura loves traveling with her family, standup paddling, perfecting the perfect brownie recipe, and reading obsessively.

She loves hearing from readers and she would love to hear from you! Send an email or connect on Facebook, Instagram, or Twitter (click the icons below).

Find me on:
www.lauradurham.com
laura@lauradurham.com

facebook.com/authorlauradurham

twitter.com/reallauradurham

instagram.com/lauradurhamauthor

Made in the USA
Middletown, DE
13 September 2019